Online Hookup: A Curvy WWBM Spicy Romance

Hunter Briggs

Published by Hunter Briggs, 2024.

This is a work of fiction. Similarities to real people, places, or events are entirely coincidental.

ONLINE HOOKUP: A CURVY WWBM SPICY ROMANCE

First edition. June 21, 2024.

Copyright © 2024 Hunter Briggs.

ISBN: 979-8224464869

Written by Hunter Briggs.

Table of Contents

Chapter 1 1
Chapter 2 4
Chapter 3 11
Chapter 4 16
Chapter 5 23
Chapter 6 32
Chapter 7 39
Chapter 8 46
Chapter 9 57
Chapter 10 61
Chapter 11 68
Chapter 12 82
Chapter 13 88
Chapter 14 92
Chapter 15 96
Chapter 16 100
Chapter 17 104
Chapter 18 109
Chapter 19 116
Chapter 20 124
Chapter 21 127
Chapter 22 132

Chapter 1

I was horny. I mean, aren't we all, but this need burned. This feeling, this want, this desire, fuck...I can't describe it. Sure I could masturbate. Hell, I've already jerked off twice today, but there's no feeling better than pussy. That soft-wet-velvet center of a woman's flesh that you simply melt in. That feeling of skin on skin contact, the magical moan in your ear while your fucking her hard and fast. That is what I want. Not some quick jerk session to porn, but a real woman with curves, holding me tightly as I make her come. That is what I want.Just thinking about it now is making me hard.

It's not that I'm ugly. Well, I don't think I am. I'm a twenty-five-year-old black man who likes working out and watching sports. I'm still in my prime, with a muscular figure, and six pack. I like shooting hoops, got a good nine to five, and I'm not tied down by a bunch of kids. I was raised right, but every man has his needs, and right now my needs were to be buried in pussy.

I didn't know what I was thinking. Hell, I'm pretty sure what I was doing was illegal somewhere, but I wanted to fuck, and fuck now. I've seen the ads online where men would post pictures of their dicks asking if anyone wanted it. I never knew if it worked. A part of me thought it was just predators, or fake pictures of women to lure men to financial scams, but I was always curious. My sexual desire drove me to the sin, and I couldn't stop myself even if I tried.

Getting naked, I laid in my bed and beat off until I became hard. My eight inches stood tall like a skyscraper, and I grinned looking at my cock. I wasn't the biggest, but the length and girth that I had definitely was a crowd pleaser.

Taking a picture of my cock, I uploaded it to the site and posted my ad, hoping that someone would see.

In the description I wrote: *Horny and looking for a hook up tonight. My preference is white and curvy, but I'm down for anything. DM for details.*

I created the ad and pressed send and patiently waited. It felt like hours until I started to get a few messages in. A few of them were bots trying to either sell me a porn subscription or a fake prostitute, that I was pretty sure was a man. I was beginning to think my efforts were futile until I got a message from a woman with a profile picture of a beautiful red head with tattoos and piercings.

Tattoogirl94: Hi, I saw your ad, are you still looking for a hookup?

Me: Yeah, are you dtf?

Tattoogirl94: of course. Are you real?

Me: Of course. Are you over 21?

Tattoogirl94: I would have to be to use this site. Plus you can see my profile picture.

Me: I know, you can never be too careful.

Tattoogirl94; Yeah, I'm 27. Wbu?

Me: 25

Tattoogirl94: Can you video chat?

Me: Yeah.

Tattoogirl94: Calling now...

My phone buzzed and I answered the call, to be greeted by the sexy redhead that I saw from before.

"Hi..." she grinned, batting her eyes at me.

"Sup..." I smirked. Just looking at her curves made my cock pulse.

"You're not half bad looking."

"Thanks, you're gorgeous. I love the tats." I replied, admiring how they covered her body.

"Thanks. Tattoos have always been a way of expressing myself."

"That's cool. I have a tattoo on my shoulder of my jersey number from when I played ball."

"That's dope. You play in college or something?"

"Nah, just high school. I wanted to play college ball, but I wasn't that great. Never got any offers and didn't want to be a walk on."

" Gotcha, so about hooking up?"

"Yeah, I'm down, but I've never done this before."

"Ah, well, I have. It's easier if we keep our real names out of it. Share as little details about ourselves as possible and just focus on the physical. It's just a hook up. Nothing more."

"Yeah, of course. So how does this work, are you coming over to my place or am I going to yours..."

"Nope. No home meet ups. Hotels only. Usually, the guys pay. I also don't do shady fifty dollar a night motel off the side of the road. Three-star hotels and up. If you can't afford that, then no sex."

"Nah, I got you. Anything else?"

"Yeah, condoms are a must. I don't care if you swear that your clean or got your shit snipped. Condoms stays on the entire time."

"Fair enough. Kissing?"

She laughed. "Yeah, kissing is cool."

"Good. When did you want to meet up, your profile says your based in Washington DC, right?"

"Yeah, I'm around that area."

"Cool, same. I can book a hotel in the area in about an hour. Did you want me to DM you the address?"

"Yes, please. I'll see you there."

I nodded. "I can't wait."

She winked at me. "See you soon."

The video call ended, and I took a deep breath as I couldn't stop from smiling. I couldn't explain why, but I had a feeling that tonight was going to be a good night.

Chapter 2

I booked a hotel at a decent chain hotel nearby, and got dressed in a nice dress shirt and jeans. Honestly, I didn't know what to wear. I mean, what do you wear to an online hook up. I made sure to grab a box of condoms on my way to the hotel and waited for TattooGirl94 in the lobby.

When she arrived, I couldn't take my eyes off her sexy curves. My cock throbbed ogling her in her strapless red top and leather skirt. Fuck me, did she look sexy. I especially loved her cherry red lipstick.

"Hi," she grinned.

"Sup."

"So, you're BasketballFan93."

"And you're TattooGirl94."

"Yep, in the flesh. Did you book the room."

"Yeah, room 530."

"Lead the way."

I nodded and walked through the lobby with Tattoogirl94 behind me. At the elevator we paused and waited for the doors to open. It was strange as I didn't know what to say to her. Normally, on a date, conversations flowed, but this one didn't. Especially considering our ground rules of not sharing personal information.

"Did you get here okay? Any bad traffic?"

Tattoogirl94 snorted, "it's DC, the traffic is always bad here."

"So true."

The elevator doors opened, and we both walked in. I pressed the button to the fifth floor and waited to be taken up. We both stared at each other, and I gave her a nervous smile.

"Sorry, this is all new to me."

"It's cool. Nervous?"

"A little bit."

"God, you're not a virgin are you?"

"No, far from it."

"Good, I would hate for it to be like like one hump and it'd would be over."

"Really? Damn that sucks. That's how it usually is from me."

"Seriously?"

"Yeah, why do you think I'm single?"

Tattoogirl94 gave me a face and I busted out laughing. "I'm just fucking with you. I'm good."

"Fuck me," she grinned, clutching her chest. "I was about to get the fuck off this elevator."

"Nah, I'm decent. Haven't had any complaints.'"

"That's good."

"I would say, with a body like yours and what you're wearing, I could see why someone could come early. You're beautiful."

Tattoogirl94 smirked at me and brushed a stranded red hair of hers behind her ear.

The doors opened and I led her towards the room. Once inside, she looked around the room.

"Decent." She nodded, taking in the view. "Seeing 495 over there is simply breathtaking..." she joked, with a smile.

I chuckled. "Right? There's a cash bar in the corner over there. Help yourself."

"Don't mind if I do. You want something?" She bent over, flashing her ass at me as she looked in the fridge. Fuck me, did she have a great ass. Just thinking about fucking her doggy made my cock pulse once more.

"Rum and coke."

"Ah, a hard liquor fan. Me too..."

"Yeah..."

She popped back up and carried, two glass, two cans of soda and the airplane bottles in her hands.

"Impressive, juggling skills. You must be a bartender." I noted.

"Ah, don't break the rule, no personal details."

"Yeah, sorry."

"It's cool. That's strike one. Get to three and I'm outta here." She replied, mixing the drinks together.

"Of course."

She handed me a glass and I groaned. "That's good. A perfect mix between the two."

"Thanks." She grinned, sipping her own drink.

"So, no personal information, huh? What are we supposed to talk about?"

She laughed. "We aren't supposed to be talking at all. This is supposed to be a hook up. Are you sure you're even dtf?"

"I am. Trust me. I just like to get to know the person I'm sticking my dick in. Come on. Amuse me."

She smirked and shook her head. "So you like basketball?"

"Yeah. Big fan of the pro team in town. You like them?"

"Yeah, big fan too. I'm always watching. We suck this year, don't we."

"We suck every year since we traded Taylor. We can barely even make the play-in playoff game."

"Yeah, we gotta fire the coach. He's terrible."

"Right? That's what I keep telling everyone, but they think it's the players."

"Nope, the problem starts from the top." She added, finishing her drink. "You almost done with that, or do I need to find you a baby bottle?"

I smirked at her, liking her sass, and finished the rest of my drink. "Pushy, pushy."

"Listen, I don't got all night."

"What you got a kid or something to get back to?"
"Strike two."
"Oh, shit, sorry."
"It's cool, just, at the rate your going, you're never going to fuck me. If you wanted to talk this much you should've joined a dating service."

I smirked and placed my glass down. I walked up towards her and towered over her. I was easily a foot taller than her as I looked down at her.

"So..."

Before she could get the words out, I placed my lips on hers and she moaned.

"You talk too much..." I whispered, in between kisses.

"Ain't that the pot calling the kettle black..."

I laughed and resumed, kissing her lips and neck. Her skin tasted sweet and my heart raced as my fingers explored her body. She pushed me back and removed her tank top to be shirtless. I groaned looking at her bare chest and lowered myself to suck her tit. She moaned as my tongue swirled around her taut nipple.

My cock grew hard and it tented in my jeans. She unbuttoned my pants and pushed down my slacks, revealing my thick girth. Reaching down she slowly jerked me off and I moaned from her tantalizing touch.

"You got a condom?" She asked.

"Yeah, over there near the bed."

"Good, get naked and put it on."

I nodded, and removed the rest of my clothes. She did the same and then laid on the bed. Breaking open the foil package, my eyes didn't leave hers as I unwrapped the condoms. Fuck me, I couldn't get over her pale curves. I loved every inch of her. From her swelled tits, to her plump belly and thick thighs. Her curvaceous body was a delight to my eyes, an appetizer for my senses, a prize that was to be had. My cock pulsed as I rolled the latex down my shaft and joined her in bed.

I kissed her once and peppered multiple kisses down her body towards her crotch.

"You don't have to go down on me."

"I want to though. Is that okay?"

She shrugged. "Go ahead."

I grinned and burrowed my face into her juicy curves. She was shaved, and I could smell her feminine musk as my tongue penetrated her folds. Damn did I love the taste of her natural lubricants. It only made me want her more.

My tongue slithered into her slit, slurping up her insides as I ate her out, she moaned, crying out her pleasures.

"Fuck me, right there. Right there..." she repeated.

I continued to tickle that sensitive spot that she liked and her screamed got louder. She thrashed in the bed, but I held her down, continuing to eat out her pussy. Fuck, did she taste good.

She was a complete stranger to me, yet, this woman's pussy was all I could think of. I didn't even know her name, yet my face was buried in her curves. Her hands slid over my shaven head, and her legs trembled, lifting higher in the air.

I pushed them back, penetrating her deeper with my tongue. Her wails were music to my ears, only making me want her more. My cock burned, yearning to be buried inside her. Damn did I want her then and there.

Pulling away from her, I stared into her eyes. "Can I fuck you?"

"Yes, please." She panted.

I adjusted my position and got on top. I slipped in with ease. She was so fucking wet. Not to mention tight. Goddamn was she tight. She felt like a fuckin' vice grip around my cock, but damn was it pleasurable.

Positing myself above her, I thrusted, taking long pumps in and out of her. She moaned every time, I sunk my cock into her.

I kissed her plump lips and she uttered, "God, you're big."

"You like it?"

"Fuck, yeah, I do. There's nothing like fucking a big black cock."

"I take it this isn't your first?"

"No, I love black men. I love y'all muscles and your cocks. Y'all know how to please a woman. That's why I answered your ad, the moment I saw your cock, I knew you'd be a good fuck."

"Yeah, I thought the same. I love curvy white woman. Your profile picture was perfect, and made me want you so bad."

"Yeah? You like bigger girls?"

"The thicker the better."

She giggled. "Can you handle a big girl on top?"

"I never thought you'd ask."

We shifted in bed, and I was on bottom while she was on top. She rode my cock, moaning loudly, and I held her pillowy hips watching the goddess before me work my cock in a way it hasn't been moved in a while. For a bigger woman, she was nimble able to twist and bounce in a variety of ways. All I had to do was lay back and watch the show, and goddamn was it a show. My favorite part was watching her ample tits jiggle. The way they swayed back and forth as she bounced on my cock was amazing.

The sights of sounds of her riding me was one of a kind. I liked watching her cum drip down my cock as she rode me, and I liked feeling her plump ass bounce off my crotch. Her skin was soft and smooth, and her lips tasted like cherry.

I groaned and shifted in the bed to get back on top. I held her legs back and blasted her, hitting her hard and fast. She cried out and closed her eyes. She took deep breaths, rubbing her tits, enjoying the pleasure I gave to her.

I was nearly there.

Seconds later, I groaned and emptied into the condom. When I was through, I pulled out of her panting.

She laid beside me, gasping for air.

"Fuck, BasketballFan93, that was good."

"I could say the same thing about you TattooGirl94."

She groaned and got up to collect her clothes.

"Where are you going?" I asked, watching her get dressed.

"This was a hook up remember,"

"Yeah, but I have the hotel room for the night. If you want to can sleep over. Maybe we can go again, then get breakfast after?"

"Don't ruin this by being clingy. I told you. This was a one time hook up. I had fun, but I gotta go."

"Wait, let's at least exchange numbers."

"Strike three."

"You can't be serious?" I sat up in bed.

"Listen, I had a good time, but let's leave this as it is. Just a one night hook up. Don't reach out to me, because I won't answer. Seriously, I did have fun though. Thanks for the good fuck." She walked towards me and kissed me.

I breathed, waiting more of her touch but she pulled away.

"I gotta go. Bye."

"Wait..." before I could say something else, she was out the door. I sighed and fell back in the bed. Call me crazy, but that was some of the best sex I had. I had to fuck her again.

Chapter 3

All I could think about was TattooGirl94. For the last couple of weeks, I've searched for her on the site, but I couldn't find her. I tried reaching out to her via DMs but none of my messages got through.

It sucked that I couldn't spend more time with her. I've had sex with multiple women before, but something about her was different. Having sex with her felt amazing. It was intimate and physical. There was passion and romance, but it was also hardcore and breathtaking. I loved the way we kissed and stared into each others eyes. We barely knew each other, but we shared so much chemistry. It sucked that she left so early, because I could see a relationship with her.

Upset I couldn't find her profile, I left my apartment and drove to get my mind off things. I didn't have a destination, I just wanted to get away. Thirty minutes down the way, I got hungry and decided to pull into a random dive bar that looked interesting.

Walking in, I made my way to the bar and sat in front of a tv., to watch the basketball game. Watching the game, I wondered where the bartender was as I was dying for a drink. Seconds later, I heard a noise from the back room and saw a woman carrying several boxes.

"Be with you in a second." Her voice sounded familiar and so did her body. Staring at her, my heart began to race believing this could be my mystery woman.

After she placed the boxes down, she turned and said, "what can I do you...." Her eyes got wide as she recognized me too.

"Shit..." she cursed.

"Hi..." I grinned.

"How did you find me? I knew it was dumb to use that site."

"No, it's not what you think. I just randomly found this place. I didn't even know you worked here."

She rose an eyebrow.

"Honest to God." I lifted my hand up as if I was a Boy Scout.

She bit her lip and shook her head. "Rum and coke?" She asked.

I nodded and watched as she made my drink. She placed it in front of me and nodded, "drink up and leave."

"Wait, what if I wanted to try the food."

"It's not that great."

"Some salesman you are."

She rolled her eyes, "what did you want?"

"Burger and fries."

She nodded and punched my order into a kiosk nearby. Afterwards, she stomped back to the boxes she was carrying and began to unload them. Damn did she look good in her black jeans, and tank top. The top show a ton of cleavage, and I assumed she showed some skin for tips, but I was happy for the show as her large breasts jiggled while she unpacked things.

I smirked, staring at her and whispered, "I never got a chance to thank you for that night."

"We're not talking about that. Bring it up again, I'll have you tossed out of here."

"Sorry." I rose my hands in defense, and sipped on my drink once more. We were both didn't speak a word until her coworker broke our spell.

"Hey, Hannah, could I get some help with table 23? I need a runner." The waiter asked.

"Yeah, on it." She replied, flipping her red hair back after unloading some straws.

"Hannah, huh?" I couldn't help but to smile finally learning her name.

"Strike one." She snapped narrowly her brow.

"We're doing that again? I thought I was already out."

She rolled her eyes and walked away. After delivering food to table 23, she stepped back behind the bar to continue to restock the supplies she brought back from the back room. I sipped my drink, staring at her wonderful ass again.

"My name is Deshawn."

"I didn't ask for it." She growled.

"I know, but it's only fair now that I know yours."

"Listen, we're not doing this. Drink your drink, eat your food, and get out. Okay?"

"Okay, okay". I leaned back in my chair and looked at the tv nearby. "Washington is winning."

Hannah didn't say anything as she continued to clean. I chuckled and took another sip of my drink.

"And now they are losing. This coach sucks."

"Are you serious?" She groaned looking up at the tv. She frowned seeing that I was lying about the score and pointed back at me. "Strike two, asshole."

"What? I had to see if you were paying attention."

She smirked at me, but didn't reply as she continued to clean. Once she was done, her and I silent both watch the game together. We didn't say much to each other, only commenting on certain players. A few minutes later, my burger came out, and I began chowing down on it. It wasn't half bad.

Halfway through my meal, another man walked in and nodded towards Hannah. He had multiple tattoos, pale skin, and combed back brown hair. To me, he looked like a biker.

The moment Hannah saw him, her eyes narrowed.

"Aren't you supposed to be watching my son?" She growled. "Tonight is your night to with him."

"He's with Kim. Calm down."

"That slut? Are you kidding me. I told you; I don't like him being watched by her."

"Maybe if you paid your half of the expenses on time, I wouldn't have to leave him with her and come down to collect. Speaking of which, you're short two hundred."

She sighed, "shit, I thought support wasn't due yet."

"I was. Two weeks ago. Pay now."

"Listen, money's tight now and..."

"What did you make in tips so far?"

"No, I need that for food and rent..."

"Should've thought about that before you slept around."

"We *both* slept around. Don't act like your God's gift to man."

"No, your just the devil in disguise. Two hundred now. Or do you want to get the courts involved and have them draft it from your bank account."

"Fuck you asshole. This is all I have." She hand him a few crumbled twenties and he counted the bills.

"That's not enough."

"I told you, it's $200. This is only $80."

Hannah glared at her ex and tears began to well in her eyes. I didn't know what drove me to do it, but I couldn't see her upset like this.

"Here..." I opened my wallet and handed the asshole the rest of the money. "That ought to cover it."

He chuckled and looked at me. "And who the fuck are you, her boyfriend?"

"No, just a man who was taught better."

"Watch you mouth..." he growled pointing at me.

"And you...pay on time next time." He walked away and Hannah closed her eyes.

"Asshole." She muttered under her breath.

I gave her a small smile and said, "sorry about that.."

"Strike three. Go leave."

"Hannah..."

"Stop..." she placed her hand up, shaking her head. "Just stop." She sighed, and narrowed her eyebrows. " I don't know what type macho shit you think you pulled back there, but I didn't need your money. Now, not only do I owe that asshole, I owe you. Please just go. Come back in a week and I'll pay you back."

"You I don't need to pay me back. I'm sorry about your ex. Families can be tough. I know I have my struggles" I pulled out a couple of twenties and tossed it on the bar. "That ought to cover the drink and burger. It was good seeing you again Hannah."

I got up and began to walk away when I heard her curse under her breath again.

"Shit, I'm sorry. You can stay. It's just, my ex... It's a sensitive topic."

"No I get it. I have exes too."

"That you share a kid with?"

"No, kids. Wanted some, but I just haven't found the right person yet."

She nodded and bit her lip. "What are you doing tonight,"

"I'm an open book."

"Stick around till close with me? I'll buy you a round after being such a dick earlier."

"Yeah, I'd like that." She nodded, grabbed a liquor bottle and poured two shot glasses. Raising a glass she said, "fuck exes"

"Fuck exes" I grinned, taking the shot.

Chapter 4

I hung out with Hannah, till after 2 am when the bar closed. During my time at the bar, she was still really reserved about certain things, especially her kid, but I didn't pry. She was a good person to chat with though. We especially connected over basketball. Turns out she used to play too in high school, so we both relived our glory days playing ball.

When the last customer was scooted out of the bar, Hannah, turned off the lights and I followed her out of the restaurant, while she locked the door behind her.

"That was fun, Hannah, thanks for the drink." I grinned.

"Where you heading?"

"Back home, why?"

"Mind if I follow you back? I need a drink. Something to mellow me out after this shit. Do you have beer at your house?"

I smirked. "Yeah. I do. Come on."

I got into my car, and Hannah got into her old jeep, and she followed my back to my apartment in Arlington. After parking our cars in the parking deck, I led her to my place, and she curiously looked around at my space on the fourth floor.

"Nice place. Must do well."

"I do okay." I smirked.

She nodded, walking around looking at the various pictures of myself with friends and family. As she looked at the pictures, I grabbed two beers and handed one to her.

"Are you a craft lager fan, that's all I have."

"You're talking to a bartender. I've drank so many beers that I'm on my second liver."

I cracked up and handed her the bottle, and she quickly snapped off the cap and tossed it in the trash.

"Impressive."

"You gotta be quick in my business. Speaking of which, what is it you do?"

"I work in finance."

"Ah, explains the degrees on the wall."

"Yeah, did you go to college?"

She shook her head. "I was lucky enough to graduate high school."

I nodded and sipped my beer once more. "Went right to work?"

"Yeah, started off working at a chain restaurant. That wasn't really paying the bills though, so I started stripping on the side."

I rose my eyebrows at her.

"Hey, I was a bit slimmer back then."

"I didn't say anything."

"Your face said it all."

"No judgement here." I grinned, drinking more of my beer.

She finished hers and I reached in the fridge for a second round. I finished my own and joined her on the second beer.

"Stripped for a couple of years, then my ex came in. He talked big game. Flashed me some dollar bills and like a fool I fell for it. One night, he fucked me without a condom and..."

"The rest is history?"

"Yeah, something like that." She sighed and drank more. "After having my son, I gained a lot of weight, and my ex, he didn't look at me like he used. It had been a while, and I wanted a quick fuck. I made one mistake, and regretted ever since."

"I'm sorry."

"It's cool. Live and learn..." she paused and looked down at her feet. "That's my story."

"That's deep. We all have our own trials. I grew up without a dad."

"Really," she asked.

"Yeah, it was just me and my mom. She made me into the man I am today."

"She did good. I can tell you got a good head on your shoulders."

"Thanks. You're a good mom."

She laughed. "No, I'm not. I only see my son three days out of the week, and I can barely pay child's support. I'm a terrible mom."

"You care. I think that matters the most. That's step one."

She smiled at me. "That's sweet. Fuck, why are you so nice? You shouldn't be slumming it with me. You should have a girlfriend or something. Why are you doing on backdoor websites looking for ass."

"Because I'm a man with needs."

"Fair enough, but seriously, why hasn't some women put a ring on that finger."

I shrugged. "I don't know. Got busy with school and work, never really paid much attention to women. I've had girlfriends in the past, but they all seem to fizzle out."

"Why is that?"

"I'm not sure."

"Fair enough." She finished her beer and watched as I finished my own drink. "Did you want to fuck? I need let out some of these frustrations from today."

"I'm a guy, I always want to fuck."

She laughed. "Condoms?"

"Yeah, I got some in my bedroom. Come on."

"Nah, she shook her head and began removing her clothes. In here. On the sofa."

I chuckled. "Okay, I'll be right back." I walked into my bedroom and grabbed a condom. When I returned back to my living room, I found Hannah, sitting on my couch, fingering herself. She was moaning loudly, plunging her fingers into her cunt.

"Started without you..." she smiled.

"It's okay, I like the view..." I grinned, admiring her tattooed pale curves. I got naked and removed the condom from the foil. After placing it on, I kneeled in front of Hannah. "Did you want me to eat you out?"

"Nah, I'm ready. Fuck me..."

I nodded, brought her towards the edge of the sofa. She giggled as she laid sprawled out in front of me. Fuck, did I love the way her pussy glistened in the limited light of my living room. I crotched down in front of her and slipped inside. Once more, I was treated to her amazing pussy.

Fuck me. I didn't know what was capturing me, but I was addicted to it. She was like a drug and all I wanted was more. I thrusted hard into her, making the sofa slide back, but I didn't care. I was in the zone, taking her. Hannah's moans sounded amazing as she wrapped her arms around my shoulders. I loved how her hands would collapse around me, rubbing and holding me tight.

"Fuck me, I missed this black cock."

"I was thinking the same about your pussy. You feel amazing."

"So do you..." she grinned. I leaned forward and kissed her and our lips stayed together in a passionate erotic kiss. Her tongue slithered across mine, the two entangled molding as one. I groan slamming myself into her with urgency.

"Deshawn?" She patted.

"Yeah?"

"Can you fuck me doggy? I want to be taken hard and fast."

"Of course." I pulled out of her and watched as she adjusted herself on the couch with her ass facing me.

"Goddamn, do I love that ass."

"Yeah?"

"Fuck, yes."

"Do you like the way I jiggle it?" She asked, twerking her rear. Honestly it was unfair. How in God's name do you make something as perfect as that.

"Yeah, damn baby it's hypnotic. An ass like that, no wonder you were a stripper."

"What can I say, I still got it."

"Damn, right you do." I slapped her ass and growled, "bring that fat ass to me. Come here."

She giggled and arched her back, allowing me to slip it in her backside. Damn, was she tight at this angle. I had to bite my lip to keep from coming early. Holding her ass cheeks I slammed into her. As I did our skin came together in a satisfying clap. Sweat rolled down my body and Hannah's ass was beet red from all the slaps I've gave her.

There was something about taking Hannah that I loved. I couldn't explain it, but it was the little things that drove my desire. I loved how soft her pale skin was, and the sound of her voice as pleasure surged through her. I loved how spicy she could be, begging me to slap her ass hard or to pull her hair. It felt like I was fucking a pornstar. All of those little things built up and I could feel my orgasm approaching.

Gasping, I came into the condom and then pulled out of her, sitting on down on the couch, clutching my chest.

"Damn, that was good." She flipped her hair back and smiled at me. Damn, could an image be any sexier? She placed her head on my sweaty shoulder exhaling loudly.

"Yeah..." I breathed, holding her close. "You have an amazing ass, by the way."

"I've been told." She laughed.

We sat for a few minutes both collecting ourselves from our prior intense affair. My hand rested on her thigh, as I softly massaged her leg.

"Did you want to stay overnight? I can make breakfast."

"No, I can't. I gotta get back. Tomorrow is night with my son."

"I gotcha. Can I at least get your number? Unless the only way you'd want me to get in contact with you is by going to your bar. You can't ghost me this time. I know where you work."

She smirked. "Yeah, sure creeper. Where's your phone?"

I got up and grabbed my jeans. Taking out my phone, I tossed it to her and she caught it.

"Nice catch."

"Played softball too."

"Figured." I snorted.

I sat next to her and unlocked my phone and gave it back to her. She looked at my profile picture of me and my mom and she smiled."you really are a mama's boy."

"Most men are."

She smiled and entered her number.

"Wait, how do I know it's real. For all I know that's a pizza place."

She laughed and pressed the send button. Moments later, her purse buzzed and she laughed, "satisfied?"

"Yeah. Not yet."

"Are you sure about that? Judging by the limp dick of yours, I've drained your balls."

"If you'd stay the night, you'd know I'll be ready for round two in an hour."

"Is that so?"

"Better believe it."

She smiled and our faces were a mere few inches a part. I wanted to kiss her but I hesitated. What was it relationship? Was it just casual sex or something more?

"Hey, what are you doing next weekend?"

"Working, like I always do."

"Yeah, but don't you get get a break?"

"My days off, I'm with with my kid."

"Oh..."

"But I can always take first shift. Why what's up?"

"Wanted to take you to dinner. You know somewhere nice where we both have to get dressed up."

"Deshawn, I like you but not like that. This is just casual sex. Nothing more. I'm not looking for a boyfriend."

"Nor am I looking for a girlfriend. Just wanted to do something outside the bedroom."

"Well, there is a DJ I like playing in DC. Want to go to that?"

"I'd love to."

"Good, I'll text you the details." Hannah got off the sofa and placed her clothes back on. Once she as clothed, she grabbed her purse and headed towards the front door. "Thanks for the beer and fuck. You know how to make a bad night better."

"Happy to be of service. If have any other sexual frustrations that you'd need to get out. You have my number now."

"Of course."

"Just to let you know this sexual therapy session was free, but the next one is going to cost you."

She laughed. "Bullshit. You and I both know, this ass was too good to charge."

"Yeah, it was."

She winked at me and blew a kiss. "I really did have a good time tonight."

"Me too. Text me when you get home safe, okay?"

"Yeah, bye."

"Bye..." I watched her walk out the door, and once she was gone, I fell back on the couch, smiling, thinking about my new friend, Hannah.

Chapter 5

Waiting outside the club I could hear the loud thump of music. I nodded my head waiting for Hannah to arrive. I knew I was early, but I couldn't help it. I was excited to hang out with Hannah again. Hanging out with her was different. She was unlike anyone else I've ever been with. I couldn't even describe it if I tired.

Looking down at my blue button down shirt and dark jeans, I hoped my outfit wasn't too much. Seriously, how do you pick out an outfit that said, I want to be friends, but I wouldn't mind if we were something more?

It wasn't too cold, which is surprising for a late March night in DC. You could tell that summer was near based on the high temperatures of seventy degrees.

A red DC taxi pulled up and Hannah walked out of the backdoor. The moment I saw her my jaw dropped. She looked amazing in her black leather mini skirt and red tank top. She had to be slightly cold with all of that exposed skin, but I'd didn't care. She looked sexy as fuck in her outfit. I loved how her breasts filled out her top, and how her mini skirt and heels highlighted her curvy thick thighs. Just looking at her my cock pulsed. Something about her just made me go wild.

"Hi..." she greeted, pushing a strand of her hair behind her ear.

"Sup..." I grinned.

She gave me a hug and I couldn't help but smile inhaling her rose perfume. Her smell made my stomach twist and for a moment I didn't want to break away from her.

"You look amazing by the way."

Her smile grew larger. "So do you." She looked away and once again pushed a strand of her hair away.

"Are ready to head in?" I asked.

"Yeah, let's go." She followed me into the club and as we ventured further in the space the music got louder. The air smelled like cheap liquor and there was a smoky haze in the damp dark room. As the bass thumped, several patrons ground on each other, moving their bodies to the beat.

Leaning closer to her I asked, "you want something to drink?"

"Yeah, rum and coke."

"You got it." I winked and left to grab the drinks. When I returned, I found Hannah rhythmically dancing to the song. I'm not going to lie, for a white girl, she did good keeping up with the pace.

"Got the drinks." I shouted, over the music.

"Awesome." She took one cup from my hand and sipped its contents.

"This DJ is really good. I love how he mixes the old school and new stuff." I yelled. My ears were pounding on how loud to was.

"Right?" She grinned, still bouncing to the beat.

"Thanks for inviting me out. This is fun."

"Yeah, I'm having a great time too. Did you see the Washington game today?"

"Yeah, we won, surprisingly we are on a hot streak. Only two games behind the tenth spot."

"If we keep this up, we can work our way into the final spot for the playoffs. March is the perfect time to get hot."

I scoffed. "You have way too much faith in DC."

"Never say never." She grinned.

"Care to dance?" I asked.

"You read my mind." She took my hand and let me towards the dance floor where there were dozens of others all moving to the beat.

We danced side by side, shimming our bodies with the rhythm. We both smiled at each other doing different dance moves. I'm not sure how long we dance and laughed together. It seemed like time stood still as we enjoyed ourselves. We started apart from one another, but inch by inch we grew closer to each other until she was grinding on my crotch.

I held her hips as her ass ground on top of me. Her head leaned back, and she held my neck as we sensually danced with one another. I could feel her breath in my skin, and my heart raced from our skin-to-skin contact. Looking down, I spied her plump tattooed cleavage. I loved the look of her tits from my perch. Feeling her body on mine, my cock pulsed, and I got hard. I think she could feel my stiffness too as she began to floss her ass over it.

I groaned feeling my cock leak precum. Damn did I want her in that moment. She grabbed my hand and brought it lower towards her crotch.

"Hannah…"

"Just go with it…" she whispered, slightly hiking her skirt, allowing me to touch her wet slit. I looked around the club to see if anyone could see our naughty deed, but everyone was consumed with themselves. Plus it was so damn dark I could barely see a foot in front of me.

"Fuck it…" I hissed slipping my finger deeper inside her. At this point, I didn't care about the public display. Her shit felt too good to leave.

"You're wet…" I whispered, softly fingering her. She moaned and pressed her body against my cock again.

"I know…did you bring a condom?"

"Yeah, why?"

"I want you."

"So do it. Did you want to leave?"

"I want it now. Come with me." She grabbed my hand and led me off the dance floor towards the bathroom. The unisex bathroom was unoccupied and Hannah pushed me in and locked the door behind her.

"We are not fucking in here. It's disgusting." I laughed, looking at the disarray room, with only a single toilet and sink.

"You got a better idea? I want you so fucking bad right now, and I'm not doing it out there in front of everyone. This is the only other option. Come on. It's just a quickie."

"What has gotten into you?" I laughed.

"Hopefully you. Don't be such a pussy. You want to get your dick wet or not?"

"You don't smell that?" I laughed.

"Smell what?" She grinned, grabbing my cock. "You're hard. I'm wet. What's the problem?"

"You think this place has every been clean?"

"Hey..."

"What," before I could say another word, she grabbed my face and kissed me. Her tongue wrapped around my own before I felt her hand slide down to my jeans. She unbuttoned me and pushed my pants and boxers down. As our mouths stayed connected as her hand grasped my hard cock. She jerked me off before squatting down in front of me and placing me in her mouth.

"Fuck..." I groaned as her tongue, slid across my pole. She lathered it in her spit, leaving it dripping before placing in her mouth again to suck it. She gurgled my cock, jerking her head back and forth, while her hand fondled my balls. I groaned, and my cock tingled from her oral pleasure.

"Fuck me..." I whispered, as my fingers combed through her hair. She gagged deep throating me, before pulling my dick out of her mouth. She gasped, as a long trail of spit was still connected to my cock and her mouth.

"You still having second thoughts fucking me? She asked.

"Not any more."

"Good." She grinned. She hiked up her skirt, and bent over the sink, revealing her juicy wet mound. "What are you waiting for then," she teased shaking her ass.

I chuckled and removed the condom from my jeans. After rolling the rubber down my shaft, I slipped inside Hannah's velvet center. She moaned, and I slapped her ass, fucking her hard.

"How's that?"

"Good...really good. Fuck me, Deshawn. Fuck me..." she moaned.

I pulled her hair back and she yelped, screaming as I gave it to her hard and fast.

"Goddamn, you're a freak."

"You like that?"

"Fuck yeah I do." I slapped her ass and smiled watching her beautiful curves jiggle once more.

"Give it to me. Give it to me..." she begged.

I growled, pumping in and out of her.

There was a bang at the door and someone yell, "yo are y'all fucking in there? What's taking so long I have to pee!"

"Fuck off!" Hannah and I both yelled at the same time.

The knocking continued as Hannah and I kept fucking.

"Don't stop. Fuck that guy." Hannah moaned.

"I'm almost there." I groaned, hold her ass cheeks.

"Keep going. Keep going. Keep ugh!" Hannah squealed and her body jolted. I felt a warm gush around my cock and I lost it. I could barely last as my thighs trembled emptying myself into the condom. When I was through, I pulled out of her and tossed the used condom in the trash.

We both looked at each other gasping for air.

"That was fun."

"Yeah it was."

There was another loud bang and the same voice yell, "yo are y'all done fucking? Can I pee now?"

"Just wait a damn minute!" Hannah snapped adjusting herself. I laughed pulling my pants up and getting dressed as well. When we finally opened the door, we saw a line outside the bathroom and several people gave us dirty looks.

"Sorry..." I grinned.

The man in front of the line flicked us off and ran into the bathroom.

Hannah and I both looked at each other and laughed, and headed towards the bar.

"Another rum and coke?" I asked.

"Yeah." She grinned.

I nodded and grabbed the bartender's attention. After getting our drinks, we sat at the bar, watching the other patron's dance.

"That was fun. I don't think I've ever done anything like that before."

"Really? I've done things like that all the time. It's not a good club experience if you didn't fuck in the club."

"What's the craziest place you've ever had sex at?" I asked.

"I'm a part of an orgy group."

"Really?"

"Yeah...it's about ten people or so. I love group sex. There nothing like getting fucked by three men."

"Wow, what was that like?"

"Exhausting, but amazing. Just when you thought the pleasure was over another guy would appear and shove his cock in your mouth or ass."

"Damn...I'm not going to lie, I've always wanted to be a part of an orgy."

"Why didn't you join one? You know the site that you found me on has groups looking for members."

I shrugged. "I don't know. I was always afraid that it would be a dude fest with like twenty guys and one woman."

Hannah laughed. "Nah, the groups are pretty selective on who they bring in. They try to keep it balance. The only way you find yourself in a room with twenty other dudes is if you got invited to a gangbang."

"Have you ever..."

Hannah laughed and slapped my knee. "Jesus, how big of a slut do you think I am."

"Coming from someone who admitted to fucking three guys at once, I don't know."

Hannah snorted and took a sip of her drink. "No, I haven't been a part of a gangbang. That's too many cocks. I draw the line at three."

"Nice to know you have standards."

Hannah winked at me, and I laughed. We both started at each other and in looked head at the tv in front of use before looking back at her.

"I wish I could experience an orgy. Just once."

"Really?"

"Yeah, I think it would be fun."

"Well, the next time I hear of one, I'll invite you."

"Really?"

"Yeah, I haven't been to one in a while. It would be good to have group sex again."

"I love how open you are with your sexuality."

"I wish my ex had your mindset. He's old school and, hated the idea polyamory."

"That's fucked up, We're all humans with urges."

"Exactly. I was still committed to him; he didn't see it that way though. Saw it as cheating. Got the courts to believe I was some sex deviant. Thus, I'm the one paying child support and only seeing my son on odd days. It's fucked up too, because he's the one that didn't do shit when he was born."

"I'm sorry."

"It's cool. Let's change the subject. I shared my sexual experiences, tell me, where's the craziest place you hooked up at?"

"I'm not as adventurous as you, but I hooked up outside while camping."

"Interesting, how was that?"

"Nice. Something about fucking in nature. Makes you feel like a caveman. Brings you back to your roots, you know what I mean?"

"Yeah I get you. I've never been one for camping."

"It's not really my scene either, but my ex liked it. She was an outdoorsy type."

"You dated a someone like that? I can't see you connecting at all with her."

"We didn't." I laughed. "We lasted two months."

"It fizzled out?"

"Yeah, all my relationships seem to trend that way." I took a sip of my drink and held a long distance stare.

"Sorry, I don't normally have any luck with men with. I mention I have a kid and they usually start running."

"That sucks. You're awesome. Kid or no kid, that shouldn't matter if you decide to date someone. Don't worry about it, you'd find someone."

"Nah, with my drama, I'm likely to stay single forever."

"No, there's someone out there for you. You funny, sexy, and a great fuck. Trust me, any guy giving you up is a fool."

She smiled at me, and then rubbed my thigh. "Thanks. You're a good friend."

I winked at her, and then looked up at the tv which showed the highlights of the Washington game.

"Hey, do you think we can hang out again?"

"Yeah, I would like that. I had fun."

"Me too. What do you think about catching a Washington game?"

"I can't afford those tickets."

"Don't worry about the tickets. I got you. Just meet me at the arena."

"Actually, do you mind picking me up? The taxi costs are crazy, and I don't have an hour to sit in the metro and wait to get to the area."

"Yeah, I got you. Just text me your address and I'll be there."

"Awesome." She grinned. She left her hand in my thigh as we continued to watch the highlights, talking about sports and life. I didn't know what the hand meant, but I'd didn't care. Being close to her was all that I wanted.

Chapter 6

Hannah didn't live in the nicest neighborhood. I wasn't surprised as rent was so damn high in NoVa area. After parking my car, I walked up to her townhouse and knocked on her door.

The brick townhouse looked like it was built in the seventies and hasn't been updated since then. The paint was chipped, and I noticed a window shutter that was hanging on by a nail. Moss grew on the brick exterior, and it looked like it badly needed to be powered washed. High grass covered the area, along with trash in neighbor yards. It wasn't the prettiest sight, and actually reminded me of the hood I grew up in.

After knocking her door, I looked down at my outfit and grinned as I was decked out in my Washington gear, wearing a flat brimmed cap, a jersey and jeans. There was no answer at first so I knocked on the door a second time and the door wasn't answered until a small boy opened it. He looked just like Hannah as his small eyes stared into mine. He had red hair and freckles with a gap tooth smile. He looked no older than five.

"Hi, is Hannah here?"

"Mama!" He yelled, walking down the hall.

"Thomas! What did I say about opening the door without me..." Hannah muttered walking towards the door and her eyes opened wide seeing me. Her red hair was in disarray, and she was wearing a baggy T-shirt, no bra, a pair of yoga pants with no make up on. It was the first time I saw her without any makeup and she looked gorgeous.

"*Shit*, Deshawn. What are you doing here?"

"The basketball game, remember? We were going to go tonight."

"*Shit*, that's tonight isn't it?"

"Yeah..."

"Fuck, I'm sorry. My ex just dropped off my son, claiming he had some where to be, even though it's his day to watch him. I'm so sorry. I meant to text you about it, but it slipped my mind. I've been so busy with Thomas."

"It's cool. Rain check?"

"Yeah, rain check. I'll see you later, okay?"

"Yeah...wait Hannah. Did you want some help?"

"Nah, I got it." On cue her kid in the background screamed and ran across the hallway. "No, running!" She snapped.

"Sorry!" The boy replied.

I laughed and looked back at Hannah. "Seriously, I don't mind. I grew up with a single mother. I know how it is, and how much y'all need breaks. I can order pizza and perhaps we can catch the game here."

Hannah smiled. "I'd like that. Come on in."

I nodded and followed Hannah into the living room. Her living room was in disarray and cluttered with toys and clothes. The set up of the room was basic, with just a fabric sofa, and two lounge chairs. In the background her flat tv, played some kids cartoon show. Her son was playing with action figures when Hannah called out to him.

"Thomas, this is Deshawn. He's one of mama's friends."

"Hi." He waved continuing to mash his toys together. I gave Hannah a small smile and sat down with Thomas, looking at his toy collection.

"Wow, I used to have this toy when I was your age."

"Do you still have it?" He asked.

"No, I lost it. Do you mind if I play with you?"

"You can play." He replied, without looking up from his toy.

I picked up a toy and acted like a bad guy. Thomas giggled and held up his toy trying to defeat mine. Hannah sat down next to us and smiled at me. Her green eyes gazed into mine before she joined us picking up a toy. We had fun playing with toys and chasing each other. When the pizza arrived, we all sat on her sofa, watching the game cheering for Washington.

Thomas didn't stay up for the entire game as he was passed out by the time the third quarter started. Hannah combed her fingers in his autumn hair, watching the young boy sleep.

"Hey, I'm going to put him to bed. I'll be right back okay?"

"Yeah, okay."

Hannah picked up her child and carried him to bed. When she returned, she smiled and sat down next to me.

"Thanks for hanging out with us, it was fun today."

"Yeah, it was. I hope I didn't impose…"

"No, I'm happy that you decided to stay. I needed some help, Thomas can be a lot sometimes. He has so much energy."

"Yeah, I get you. I used to be the same. Have you thought about sports? My mom put me in basketball, around his age."

"I would if I could, but my ex has him for a lot of the time, so it would be hard to take him to practice and stuff."

"I get you. Perhaps that something you could talk to him about?"

"You've met my ex. You know much of an asshole he could be."

"True, but it's for your kid. His first priority should be him."

"You'd think, but I think his priorities shifted to just collecting child support from me."

"Asshole."

"Right?"

The game returned from commercial, and Hannah laid back onto my shoulder. "We're still winning?"

"Yeah, 85-83. It's a tight game."

"We'd pull through."

"You'd think?"

"Yeah."

"I don't know. Detroit's defense is good. They can come back and win it."

"Aren't you supposed to be a Washington fan? You have little faith."

"I am a fan; it's just I don't live in a fantasy land. Detroit is the best team in the nation. This was going to be a tough win."

"Such a fair-weather fan."

"No, I just recognize game."

"Nah, you're just a bandwagon fan."

I laughed. "A bet then."

"Go on..."

"If Washington wins, I'll eat you out. And if Detroit wins, you'll suck me off. Deal?"

She laughed. "Deal. By the way, I'm sitting on your face."

I chuckled. "You're really confident, but that's not going to happen because you're going to lose. When I win, I expect you to swallow."

"I always do." She winked. Damn was the smirk sexy as hell. I don't know why but looking at her smile made my cock pulse.

It felt weird cheering against my team, but honestly I really wanted some head. Getting blown was a higher priority than my team winning, and if you're against that, then you've obviously never gotten good head before.

It was fun watching and cheering on the game with Hannah. She was so competitive, pushing me and talking trash. I loved it. It was like she was one of the boys, and it made the game more interesting.

With ten seconds left in the game, Detroit was winning by two, 111 to 109. Washington had the ball had it on Detroit's side.

"Washington is going to miss this three." I grinned.

"We're going to hit it."

"Nah. Detroit's going to block this shot. They have the best defense in the league. Fuck, I might as well get ready now." I unbuttoned my jeans and lowered them to floor. I stroked my cock, getting it hard for it to stand upright.

She laughed and looked back at the game. I watched as the clock counted down to zero and with one second left in the game,

Washington shot a deep three. When the ball dropped in the net, Hannah jumped up and shout, "Boom! We win! 112 to 111! Pull you pants up, and sit back to take this pussy!"

"What? Bullshit! He didn't get the shot off."

The replay proved me wrong was the ball clearly was out of the players hands before the clock struck zero.

"You were saying?" She smirked.

"Fuck. Well, a deal is a deal. Come here girl." I laid back in the sofa, waiting for her to sit on top of me.

She giggled and removed her yoga pants. I grinned, looking at her thick pale thighs, and watched as she straddled my face. Smelling her musk, I groaned, and my cock twitched from her erotic scent. Holding her smooth curves, my tongue slipped inside her slit and slithered in and out of her. She moaned and ground her ass into my face. I groaned, slurping up her wetness, sucking on supple fleshy lips.

"Fuck...." She groaned.

I could barely breathe with her weight on top of me, but that only turned me on more. My cock burned from being so damn hard. I soon felt a hand clasp around my cock, and I could feel Hannah jerking me off. Seconds later her mouth collapsed around my cock, and felt her licking and sucking my dick.

My body trembled from the erotic tingle going through me. I moaned on her pussy as she too provided me pleasure. I heard her gag and cough, deep throating me, and she proceeded to jerk my slick cock with her hand.

"Are you going to come for me?"

"Mmm..." I managed to mumble.

"Yeah, did you want me to swallow it?"

"Mmm..." I grunted once more.

Hannah placed me in her mouth again and her suction felt amazing. I loved how she rolled my balls in her hands and how rapidly she jerked me off. The way her tongue licked the tip of my penis, and the sounds of her gurgling my cock.

Hannah moaned loudly and her body shifted. She took deep breathes gasping for air.

"Right there, right there. Fuck me. Oh fuck...." She muttered. I held onto her sweaty thighs tasting her come. That salty nectar made me groan, only turning me on more.

Seconds later I came too. I groaned loudly as my cock pumped loads of cum into Hannah's mouth. She swallowed, and licked the remaining residue off my cock.

She then slid off of my face, allowing me to get fresh air.

"Damn that was wonderful."

"Yeah, it was." She grinned.

"You sucked me off. I thought I lost."

"You did, but I couldn't stand looking that your hard cock without touching it. Hope you didn't mind."

"No, not at all. You're right, you do give good head."

"Thanks."

"Did you want to go again?"

"Did you bring any condoms?"

"No, sorry. Do you have any?"

"No."

"Oh, I could run out and get a box."

She sighed and looked at her watch. "No, actually it's getting late. Perhaps we call it a night."

"You sure? I don't mind staying over."

"Yeah, I really don't feel like explaining to my son, why you stayed the night. We already took a big step today. Let's not push it."

"Yeah, I got you. I really did have fun today. I wouldn't mind hanging out with you and Thomas again."

"Deshawn, I don't think that's a good idea. I don't want Thomas getting attached to you, then you leave and I have to explain to him why."

"Oh..."

"Yeah. We can still hang out, but let's just leave him out of this."

"Okay, sure."

"I really did have a good time today."

"Same." She grinned.

"When are you free again?"

"I'll have some time on Tuesday. It's my day off from work."

"I work that day, but that night if you want to get a drink we can."

"Yeah I'll like that ."

I smiled and pulled up my pants, and zipped them up. "See you then?"

"Yeah, see you then."

I leaned forward and gave Hannah a hug and walked to the door.

"Hey, Deshawn?" Hannah called out.

"Sup?"

"I really do appreciate you as a friend. Thanks for this."

"You're welcome, but we're more than friends."

"What?" She gawked.

"We're fuck buddies."

She relaxed once she understood my joke and laughed. "Damn straight. See you soon. Fuck buddy."

"See you later, buddy." I winked, walking out the door.

Walking to my car, I sighed. Don't get me wrong, I was happy to be friends with Hannah, but a part of me wanted to be something more with her. Was I falling for Hannah?

Chapter 7

Hannah moaned sipping the wine in the steak house. The restaurant was a white linen , bow-tied server type of establishment. The room was dimly lit, with only a few candles on the tables giving it an intimate vibe

As she continued to moan from the taste of her wine, I grinned. There was something about the sound of her moan that got me hard. I couldn't describe it even if I could. Perhaps it was like a pavlov dog theory situation, where just the simple sound made me salivate. In this case her moans made me hard.

"Damn, this wine is good."

"Yeah, it is."

"You know you didn't have to take me to this fancy place. We're just friends. This isn't a first date or something."

"I know, I know." I grinned. "It's just I didn't want to eat at a chain place, do you blame me? Tell, me did you like your steak or not?"

"No, don't get me wrong, the steak was amazing. I didn't know meat could melt in your mouth like that, but I can't afford a $70 steak."

"Don't worry about it. I'll pick up the tab."

"Typical guy. Well, don't expect me to put out."

"Please, you were going to put out regardless of how this night went."

"Really?" She scoffed.

"Yeah, you love my black cock."

She choked on her wine and coughed, while laughing. "Damn, Deshawn."

I chuckled and sipped my wine.

She wiped her face with the white linen napkin and smiled back at me. "Tell me the truth, what's the real reason you took me here?"

"Isn't it obvious? I wanted to get you into a sexy dress. You look stunning by the way," I admired her sequin black dress, with a low v cut, and a high slit on her upper thigh showing off her tattoos on her legs and breasts. She wore ruby red lipstick and her red hair rested on her shoulders as she looked down and smiled at me.

"You look good too."

"This suit? Nah I wear a suit every day at work. This is nothing.""

"To me it's nice. Most of the men in my line of work are wearing biker jackets and jeans. It's nice."

"Thanks. Did you want desert?" I asked.

"Don't tempt me with a good time. Of course I want dessert, do think think they have crème brûlée here? That's my favorite dessert?"

"I think I did see it on the menu. I'll order it." I flagged down the waiter and asked for the dessert along with two spoons. Once the waiter was gone, I looked back at Hannah and smiled, "thanks for hanging out with me tonight. I had fun."

"So did, I but why are you acting like this night is over? My ex has Thomas tonight."

"Yeah, but you typically don't stay the night. It's getting late, plus I have to work tomorrow."

"Oh…okay; it's cool…" she smirked, placing her hand on her chin, giving me this sexy devilish look. "I figured, since you we were going into a fancy restaurant like this and you were paying, I could at least repay you by sleeping over and fucking you." Her eyes fluttered, and I then felt her bare foot, slide down my leg. My cock twitched from her touch, and I breathed deeply looking into her green eyes. Fuck me, I was under her spell. "…but if you have to go to work…I completely understand."

"Fuck work. I'll call in sick."

She chuckled. "Willing to throw it all away for a quick fuck?"

"A quick fuck with you is worth it."

She laughed. "Damn, it's true what they say, a woman's curves is powerful."

"They're damn right unfair. Especially your curves. Fuck me, I'm not sure how one woman could be so sexy."

She shook her head and finished her glass. "I'm going to need more wine."

"Same..." I grinned, finishing my own glass.

We finished our wine and dessert and then left the restaurant. Driving down the highway, I looked at Hannah and asked, "my place or yours?"

"Yours." She replied. "I hate my place. Yours is so much nicer."

"Hey, your townhouse isn't that bad."

"Don't kid yourself. Besides the gunshots and the drunk assholes stumbling down the streets my neighborhood is a complete dream. I live in a shit neighbor in the projects."

"Hey, I grew up on a street like that. The streets made me into a man, thought me how to scrap and taught me how to be a man. You got a roof over your head, that's what counts."

She shrugged. "I just wish I could have a place like yours."

"It's a'ight. The rent is ridiculous though. For the amount I pay, I could easily afford a mortgage."

"Why don't you get a house?"

"Just for me? Nah, apartments are easier to maintain. It's just me, I don't have to worry about up keep or cutting the grass."

"Is that supposed to be a shot, towards me? I know I haven't cut my grass in a while."

I laughed, "not at all, but if need help, give me a call."

"I'm good. You're my fuck buddy not my handy man."

"Ah, come on, it could be a fantasy. I'll take my shirt off, you can be the sexy milf whose husband is out of town and you're cheating on him with the help?"

"Milf? How old do you think I am?"

"You are a milf, you're a fuckable mom..."

"Oh, fuck I am." She rubbed her face in her hands laughing.

"Hey, don't get upset. I love that I'm fucking a milf."

"You would. You're such a freak."

"You know it." I winked, I reached over and rubbed her thigh, giving her a smile.

She smiled back at me and grabbed my hand.

"Hannah, what are you..." I took my eyes off the road and watched as she hiked up her dress slightly.

"I'm not wearing any panties. Want to see?"

I nodded and my hand slide up her upper thigh towards her center.

Fuck, was she wet, as my finger slipped into her cunt. She moaned and circled her hips, riding my finger as if it were a cock. It was hard to keep my eyes on the road as Hannah moaned riding my hand. She rubbed her tit through the dress and groaned, her lip quivered as her pleasure increased.

"Fuck..." I uttered. I was between a rock and a hard place as all I wanted to do was watch her get off, but I was driving sixty miles per hour down the highway and my eyes couldn't be diverted.

My cock tented in my slacks, and I could feel the precum leaking in my boxers. Between her moans and the feeling of her slick pussy, my shit was harder than stone.

"Looks like someone wants to play too. Want me to help you?"

"Yes, please..."

Hannah grinned, and removed my hand from her crotch. Leaning close to me, she unzipped my slacks, and slipped her hand inside my boxers. She pulled out my cock and started jerking me off.

"Fuck..." I muttered. My hands trembled and we swerved slightly into the other lane.

A car behind us honked and Hannah laughed, "don't get us killed."

"Sorry. It would be a hell of a way to go though right?"

"Yeah, but I think this would be better..." she unbuckled herself and leaned down to place my cock in her mouth. Her head bobbed up and down, sucking me off while I drove. It was even harder to concentrate with her mouth around me. Her hair tickled my arm as her head rubbed my arm, and my vision was slightly impaired by her constant bobbing head, but I could complain, her blow job felt amazing.

We got off the highway and I stopped at a light towards my apartment complex. Waiting for the green light, another car stopped by me. There was an older man driving and a older woman sat in the passenger side. The older woman looked at me and gasping shaking her head. Getting the older man's attention, he looked over at me and and winked.

I gave him a nervous laugh and wave while his spouse slapped him. Thankfully the light turned green and I drove away from the awkward scene.

"What's so funny?" Hannah asked, pushing her hair back.

"It appeared we had an audience at the light."

"Oh..." she laughed. "Well, at least we gave them a show."

"Yeah, we did." I grinned.

We drove into the parking deck and I parked the furthest distance I could away from my apartment .

"Why did you park so far?" Hannah asked.

"Because, I couldn't wait to get back to my apartment to have you. I reached into my center console and brought out a box of condoms". After last time, I made sure to always have a box on me. Want to start the fun here?"

She laughed. "Of course."

I pushed the seat back, while she hiked her dress up to her stomach. Taking the condom out, I rolled the latex down my shaft and Hannah hopped on. Hold her ass, I groaned as she rode me. Our lips connected in an erotic kiss. As our tongues twisted around each other she moaned.

"Yeah; that's it. Take me. Take me." I growled slapping her ass.

Hannah cried out, holding the headrest as she bounced wildly up and down. The car shook and squeaked from her movements. I slapped her ass several times before grabbing her ass cheeks and pounding into her.

She screamed, begging me to fuck her harder and faster. I was in the zone while I took her. I didn't care if someone caught us or if we got in trouble. I only wanted her. She was mine in that moment.

Watching her ride me, she looked like a goddess. She looked so damn sexy in her black dress. I loved the way her tits bounced in it, and I loved the feeling of the fabric rubbing against my belly. I could smell her perfume as her neck was close to my nose. It drove me mad, making me want to lick her soft pale skin and suck on it. How can skin taste so sweet? I sucked on her for so long that I left my mark on her. Good. I wanted everyone to see that I was the one who took her. I was claiming her. She was a fucking mine.

That feeling of her pussy around my cock. Fuck, it was hard just to put into words. How do you describe perfection? It was everything I wanted. The tight and wet combination was addicting, and all I wanted was more.

Sweat rolled down our foreheads from our strenuous affair. The windows fogged up, and the air smelled foul form our musks. We didn't stop though. We were both driven by a basic need. A need of pleasure.

I slapped her ass once more and growled, "fuck, I'm going to come."

"Then do it baby. Fucking finish in me."

I groaned and felt my cock spurt inside her. When I was through, Hannah held me tightly and smiled.

"Wow, that was good. You couldn't wait to have me could you?"

I laughed, "what can I say, that dress, those curves, those heels, baby you have a hold on me. You got me under your spell, and you can tell me to jump, I'll simply ask how high,"

"Ah, a woman's pussy. It can make a man do anything."

"Damn straight…" I grinned. "This was fun wasn't it."
"It was. Come on, let's head inside."

Chapter 8

Hannah followed me into my apartment and tossed her purse down onto my nearby sofa.

"I'm sure you're dying to get out of that dress. Let me get you some pjs. Follow me to my bedroom."

"Not the worst pickup line I've heard to bring me to a bedroom."

"What's the worst."

"Did you want to fuck?" She laughed.

"What's wrong with that?"

"Blunt and too direct. Make it fun."

"Noted." I smirked, walking into my room. Opening my closet I grabbed an old jersey and tossed it towards her.

"You can't be serious..." she laughed.

"What?"

"A jersey? What are we in high school?"

"Listen, it's the only thing long enough to go past your hips. I have shirts, but I don't think they'd go past your waist. Did you want to wear my boxers?"

"Nah, I'll freeball it."

"That's tempting." I smirked.

"Could you get your mind out of the gutter for a minute."

"Never."

She laughed shaking her head. "Can you do me a favor?"

"Yeah?"

"Unzip me?" She turned her back towards me, and I approached her. My heart raced ogling her soft pale back. The moment my fingers touched her skin it felt this electric spark between us. We've had sex dozens of times, yet I still can't shake this feeling as if this was my first time ever touching her. I unclasped the locket and lowered the zipper down towards her mid-back.

"Thanks…" she shimmed out of the dress, revealing her naked body. "I just wanted to take a shower before getting in my pjs."

"Okay cool. I'll wait for you to start the movie."

"You're not joining me?"

"I didn't think I was invited."

"You're always invited…" she gave me a sultry look and shook her ass as she headed towards the bathroom.

"Fuck me…" I muttered. I quickly removed my clothes and followed her into the bathroom, where she was warming up the water.

"Ah, I'm glad you decided to join me."

"I'd never miss out on a chance to look at those tits."

She snorted and laughed. "You are so corny. Come, wash me off."

I nodded and joined her in the warm steamy shower. She stood under the warm water, while I lathered my hands in soap, and spread the soapy water all over her body. I love the feeling of her soft wet body. I made sure to wash every inch of her, and she did the same, spreading the soapy all over my body. She made it a priority to jerk off my cock.

My cock pulsed and got hard. Like a zombie it arose from its dormant position and jutted out from my body. I loved watching her red painted finger nailed hand rub my cock. There was something pleasing to the eye as her pale hand wrapped around my black cock. Soap suds covered and dripped off my dick, and I smiled at Hannah, before grabbing her chin and kissing her.

She moaned, and continued to stroke me.

"Wanna have shower sex?" I whispered.

"No, I can't in here. Condom remember?"

"Yeah. Sorry." I breathed, attempting to keep my urges at bay. "You're such a fucking tease…"

"I know…" she gave me a naughty glance and shook her ass on top of my cock.

"Damn, girl..." I growled and pushed her back onto the tile of the shower wall, and sucked and kissed her neck. She gasped, titling her neck, giving me greater access.

"If I were a lesser man, I would have you right here. I would have you against the wall, and I'll be fucking taking you. Goddamn. You're so fucking sexy right now." I muttered, touching her shoulders.

She shuddered at my touch.

My cock tingled as it was only a mere inch away from her opening.

I kissed her once more and backed away. It took all of my power to do that. Fuck me, was she a tease.

She grinned at me, and it was likely she was just as turned on as I was from our little session in the shower. "Are you ready to get out?" She asked.

I sighed and nodded. "Yeah, I'm good."

Hannah reached behind her and turned off the water, and we both stepped out. Grabbing a towel from my linen closet nearby, I tossed one to her, and then used another one to dry myself off. Hannah and I grinned at each other, and she bit her lip.

"I know this is a dumb question, considering you're black and you barely have any hair, but you would happen to have a hairdryer?"

"Yeah, my ex left one here. Let me grab it."

"Cool thanks. Oh, and bring the jersey too."

"Yep," I walked into my bedroom closet, and grabbed the hairdryer along with the jersey and walked back into the bathroom. Hannah had a towel wrapped around her large breasts when I came in.

"It's a shame you cover those."

"You want a little show?"

"Once again you tease me."

"Oh, you haven't seen nothing yet," she winked, dropping her towel.

"Fuck me..." I uttered looking at her pale plus size curves. Her tattooed body had me under a spell that I couldn't break free from.

There's a reason why women with her body type are called bbws. Everything is big, including her ass and tits, plus everything about her is beautiful.

She winked at me and then plugged in the hairdryer, to dry her hair. As she blew the hot air into her hair, I yelled over the noise, "hey, did you want another drink?"

"Yeah, I would love one." She responded at equal tone.

"You want straight rum?"

"Yeah, that's fine." She shouted back.

I nodded and left the bathroom. In the bedroom, I opened my dresser and grabbed a pair of grey sweats, and placed them on. I didn't bother with a shirt as I always slept shirtless. Walking into the kitchen, I grabbed two glasses, and a bottle of rum, and poured two fingers worth of liquor in both. Placing the cap back on the rum, I placed the bottle back on the shelf on my little bar set up, and took a sip of my drink.

In the background I could hear the hairdryer shut off and shuffling in my bedroom. I was curious on what she was doing in there, and headed back into my room, with the drinks in my hand.

"Hannah, are you okay..." my voice trailed off the moment I saw her sitting in my bed, looking through my black box of sin. Hannah laughed as she took out the multiple porn dvds and my pocket pussy.

"Well, it looks like you found my porn collection." I mumbled slightly embarrassed.

"It's cool, every guy has one. You know can tell a lot from what a guy watches in porn."

"And what can you tell about me?" I smirked feeling a bit more confident.

"Let's see, when it comes to sex, you're pretty vanilla, there's no freaky bondage stuff in here. However, I see you do have a thing for interracial sex, featuring black men. I don't see any porn here where the male is any other race besides black, and none of the females are black either."

"What did you expect?" I chuckled. I handed her the glass of rum and replied, "go on..." I replied, sitting on the bed next to her.

"Hmm, let's see..." she muttered, taking a sip of rum. "You're mostly into milfs, housewives, and matures..."

"Yeah, call me strange, but I prefer an older women with curves. Saggy tits and all."

Hannah laughed, and shook her head, "plus you're not afraid to watch some bbw porn." She waved three dvd covers of busty bbws in my face.

"Nope. I love chubby women."

"I'm starting to see why we hang out so much."

"What can I say, I have a type. You're perfect."

Hannah blushed and looked down. She cleared her throat and took another sip of her rum. She shuffled through my porn collection and then laughed.

"What?" I asked.

"I forgot one more thing. It appears you have an Asian fetish as well."

I snickered. "I wouldn't call it a fetish. I just like Asian women too. I think they're beautiful."

"Sure..." she gave me a skeptical look before she continued to dig through the box. "Damn, how many pocket pussies do you have in here."

"Listen, each one of those are different molds from porn stars."

She laughed loudly and covered her face. "Damn, you really were desperate when you reached out to me."

"No, I just have a high sex drive, that's perfectly normal."

"No, having this many sex toys isn't."

"What, you don't have a collection of dildos at home?"

"I only got one, usually if I want sex, I'll find it. I have a little black box hidden in my closet. Well in this case, big black box."

"Judgy much?"

Hannah laughed and slapped my shoulder. "I'm just fucking with you."

I shook my head, smiling. Taking another sip of my rum, I watched her pull out more stuff from my box.

"Whoa, you swing both ways or something?" She asked, taking out an unopened box of anal plugs.

"Oh, no, not at all. I bought those for my ex and me, we wanted to try anal, but she got cold feet, and since the porn shop I go to has a no return policy, I'm stuck with a box of unused anal plugs."

"Wait, so you never tried anal before?"

"No, I wanted to, but never found a woman down for it."

"I'm down. I would love to take your anal virginity."

"Wait, are you serious?"

"Yeah. I don't mind anal. Plus, we already took a shower, and these plugs haven't been used yet. Are you down?"

"Fuck yes..."

"You got lube?"

"Yeah..." I rolled in my bed and reached into my nightstand drawer to bring out a bottle.

"Perfect. Move the stuff off the bed."

I nodded and hastily pushed everything off the bed. As I did, Hannah downed the rest of her drink and placed it on the nearby nightstand. I finished the rest of mine and placed my glass near hers.

"Okay," she breathed, "we have to do this slowly. Start with a lubed finger, opening me up, and then we put the plug in. Okay?"

"Yeah, I got you."

She nodded and got on all fours with her ass in the air. "Okay? Go ahead finger me..."

I smirked and poured lube on my index finger and then approached her pink puckered hole. It was a sight to see, I loved looking at her plump white ass, and her pink pussy, just south if her asshole. I bit my lip approaching her and then slowly stuck my finger inside her.

My finger got sucked inside her, and she moaned from my intrusion.

"Go slow, remember. Let my body open up. Don't be afraid to use a lot of lube." She whispered with her face down in the mattress.

I nodded and slowly moved my finger back and forth. As I worked her hole, I added more lube to my finger, greasing up her tight crevice until my finger was able to easily slide in and out.

"Fuck me...that's it. Work it open."

Sure enough, her tiny cavity began to widen.

"Add another finger," she grunted.

"Does this hurt?"

"There's some pain. Helps if you rub my pussy."

I nodded and with my opposite hand I fingered her. She moaned and closed her eyes while I worked both my hands inside her.

She breathed deeply and moaned, "okay, I'm ready, add the plug. Make sure that shit is greased."

I nodded and lubed up the black silicone anal plug and then slipped it into her gaping hole. She squealed as I slid the plug inside her.

"You okay?"

"Yeah I'm good." She whispered. She closed her eyes, and her body trembled. "You're getting the plug in your ass after this..." she teased.

"Ha-ha...What?"

"Kidding. A little anal humor. Give me a few minutes. Let the plug stretch me out."

"You still in pain?"

"It's okay, it's like this pleasurable pain."

"I could eat you out while we wait."

"That would be wonderful."

"Spread your legs."

Hannah made an opening of me, and I shuffled onto my back and held her thighs while she sat on my face. Once again, her pussy covered my face, and once again I was in heaven, as I slurped on her insides. My tongue slithered in and out of her and Hannah moaned, enjoying my oral pleasure. I made sure to tease her clit with my mouth, sucking on her delicate bud. This sent her over the edge as she cried out.

"Fuck me…. Oh fuck…" her body trembled and I tasted her come.

"Deshawn?"

"Yeah?"

"Can you fuck me? Press down on the plug while you fuck me doggy."

"Yeah sure."

"Don't forget the condom."

"Yeah, I got you."

I rolled underneath her and removed my sweats. Grabbing a condom from my dresser, I rolled the latex down my shaft and hopped back onto the bed with her. Hannah was fingering herself while she waited.

"How bad do you want this dick?"

"Badly…" she moaned.

"How bad?"

"Badly. Please fuck me…" she begged.

I laughed and slipped in my cock. Taking her by the ass, I fucked her hard and fast, making sure to press the anal plug in. She screamed out in pleasure, pulling bedsheets as her body rocked back and forth.

From my POV it was amazing. I love the way her chubby pale cheeks clapped against my stomach. Her puckered hole was covered by the black silicone plug, while my cock covered condom was drenched in her juices. Damn was it picturesque.

I slapped her ass hard and asked, "how does that dick feel?"

"Good."

"How does it feel?"

"It feels good!" She yelped.

I laughed and massaged her ass, with my hands, watching her fat jiggle. I slapped her rear once more memorized by the way her body moved.

"Ugh...I think I'm ready." She gasped.

"Yeah?"

"Yes, change out your condom. Put a lot lube on there, and don't go too deep. You're big, so it can't take all of you."

"Okay."

I pulled out of her and switched condoms. Grabbing the bottle of lube, I drenched my cock with the clear lubricant and stroked my stiffness, making sure every inch of me was covered. When I climbed back into the bed, I approached Hannah, and removed the plug to see her gaping hole. Her pink asshole was wide enough for my dick to slip in and in one breath I muttered, "fuck me..." it was a glorious sight.

Taking a deep breath, I approached her rear, and slipped inside her tight cavity. The shit was tighter than imagined. It felt like someone was squeezing my cock with their hand, and Hannah screamed as I sunk each inch into her.

"Fuck...fuck...fuck. Go slower. Go slower..." she breathed.

I nodded and adjusted myself.

"Okay, okay, that's enough. Pull out."

I followed her instructions and got out of her.

"Add more lube and go slower this time."

"Okay," once more I painted my cock in the wet substance and then entered her again. Slowly, I dipped into her and she moaned again.

"Okay, I'm good. Go head and thrust a little faster."

I nodded and began to move my hips rhythmically. She moaned on the sheets and her body quivered.

"Yeah that's it. That's it. That pace is good." She groaned.

I nodded and kept the same speed. It felt amazing to be in her ass and honestly I didn't know how long I would last being in that tight space. As I fucked her, I watched her rub her clit. Her moans of pleasure was music to my ears as I took her.

"Yeah, that's it. That's it…fuckkk…" she uttered.

Her hand moved with urgency, fingering herself with blistering speed. Above her hand, my cock, slipped in and out of her puckered pink hole. Once more I was granted a beautiful sight of my cock being swallowed by her ass. There was nothing like seeing my black cock between her fat white cheeks.

I smiled and felt my balls tingle. I knew I couldn't last any longer. I was nearly there.

Biting my lip, I groaned filling my condom up with cum, and I didn't stop fucking her until I was limp. When I was through, I gasped and pulled out her.

Pulling off the condom, I tied it and tossed it in the trash nearby and laid down in the bed, still gasping for air. Hannah rolled to her back, placing her hand on her forehead. Her brow was sweaty and her red hair was matted to her face as she took long winded breaths.

"How was your first anal experience?" She asked.

"Amazing. You are simply amazing…" I grinned, I rolled over and kissed her.

"What was that for?" She asked.

"A tip for a job well done."

"I like it." She grinned. She rolled over and kissed me. "Thanks for making me come. Damn do I love that black cock of yours."

I laughed. "We're two peas in a pod right,"

"Yeah, I'm happy you're my friend."

The word hit stronger than I expected. I knew what we were and was okay with it, but hearing the word friend felt strange.

"I am too." I replied back, but I was unsure of what I was saying had any truth at all.

"Good night…" she replied, placing her arm on my chest.

"Night..." I held her tightly looking up at the ceiling wondering if these feelings were real or not.

Chapter 9

Waking up, I found Hannah's arm and leg draped over my body. I grinned staring at her beautiful curves. I know I've said this several times, but there was nothing sexier than her. I loved how her red hair matted her face, and how plump lips quivered as she snored softy.

Wearing only my jersey, I spied her upper thick thigh that was laying across me. I love how the jersey covered her body, leaving just a glimpse of her ass cheek that was hanging out.

Laying there, my cock still was sore from its experience last night. I loved fucking her anally. I don't know why, but sex with her is such an adventure. Every time I'm with her, it feels like the first time. She was open, making the sex ten times better, I feel like anything I wanted to do she was down for. None of my prior exes were like this. With Hannah it felt like we were always ready to go, either in the bathroom at the club, in the car or living room. She certainly made my life amazing. She was like no other woman I've ever been with.

It was a shame we're just friends, because I knew if we were together, our lives would never be dull. A part of me wanted to tell her how I felt. I wanted to be hers and she'd be mine. I had this fantasy of us getting together, and buying a house. Her and Thomas could move with me, we'd be a happy family just to the three of us, and on the nights where it was just Hannah and me alone we would make passionate love, fucking everywhere we could.

I sighed, I don't know what's wrong with me. I mean how could a simple online hook up turn to this? Was I a fool to think that there could be something more than what we have? What we had was good, and getting serious in a relationship could only ruin it. In my past experiences, my relationships always run their course. Perhaps it's better that we just keep our separate ways, and just keep to fooling around.

Or...I shivered at the thought.

I could man up and tell her how I really feel. Put the cards on the table and say, let's be more than this. Let's be exclusive...

Exclusive what does that even mean to a person like Hannah?

Deep in thought, I watched Hannah's eyes flutter and open. She stared at me and smiled.

"You're gawking at me..." she whispered.

"Sorry, it's just. You're beautiful when you snore."

"Oh, god, your one of those people."

"What?"

"The ones who watch someone sleep."

"No, I just happened to wake up before you."

"Sure..." she grinned.

"Hey, Hannah...can I ask you a question?" I breathed. I didn't know what she was going to say, but I had to tell her my feelings.

"Yeah, hold that thought I have to pee..." she rolled out of bed and briskly walked towards the bathroom. Fuck me, even her walk in that jersey was sexy. Was there no better sight than seeing a woman's ass, jiggle? I waited for a few moments, before I heard the water flush and Hannah emerge from the bathroom.

"I'm sorry, you were saying?" She asked at the doorway.

"Yeah, I wanted..." before I could say another word, Hannah's phone rang.

"Shit, I'm sorry, let me get this, it could be something with Thomas."

"Okay..."

Hannah stared at the number and tilted her head back, "huh...not Thomas. Let me take it though. Sorry."

"No, it's cool."

Hannah unlocked her phone, and replied, "hello,"

I couldn't hear the caller, but I pieced together the conversation based on what Hannah's was saying.

"Huh...yeah...yeah, it would be just the two of us..."

She winked at me and then looked down at the mattress.

"No, no, no, he's not my boyfriend. Just fuck buddies...

My heart lurched as she confirmed our status. She didn't even blink an eye saying it. What was I thinking. To her, we'd always be that.

Her smile doubled, and she shook her head, "yeah, yeah, I think I'm free that day. Yeah, I don't know, let me ask."

Hannah looked at me, "what are you doing Sunday?"

"Nothing why?"

"We just got invited to an orgy. Are you in?"

I rose my eyebrows speechless. "Yeah, I'm in."

"Cool." She focused back on her call and replied, "yeah, he's in. Of course, you'd love him. Muscular black guy, big cock, good endurance. I wouldn't invite him if he was trash. He's just green when it comes to orgies. Never been a part of one." She snickered, "yeah, we'd be popping his cherry. Okay, okay , yeah. I'm excited too. Talk you you later. Bye."

Hannah hung up the call and rose her eyebrows. "Hey remember our conversation at the club about how you wanted to be a part of an orgy?"

"Yeah."

"Well, Deshawn, I hope your ready for the first orgy because we're having one this Sunday."

"Nice..." those were the only words I was able to get out.

"Ugh, I expected you to be more excited. Especially after our talk the other day on how you wanted to be involved in one. I reached out to my friends, and they wanted you a part of their next one."

"I am excited. Don't get me wrong, it's just..."

"What?"

"Nothing...just nervous. It's my first time."

She laughed, "since when do you get cold feet. You'd be fine. Trust me. You passed the trials of fucking me. If you can handle me, you can handle the others at the orgy. It's pretty much like watching porn, but more surreal."

"Gotcha."

She smiled at me and then gasped. "Oh, what did you want to tell me? I totally forgot you wanted to talk."

"Oh, it's nothing." I shook my head, "I just wanted to tell you that you look sexy in the jersey."

"Yeah," grinned, modeling the outfit for me. "Did you want another go in it? I'm in the mood for some morning sex."

"Yeah, come here."

Hannah giggled and straddled my waist. I held her hips looking into her green eyes.

"Are you sure you're okay?"

"Of course. Just hungry."

"Actually, I am too..."

"Change of plans, we order some delivery, and while we wait, we get a quickie in."

Hannah, laughed, "and that's why we're friends. Come here you." She dragged my face towards hers and kissed me. As we made out, the last word she said, rung in my head. Friends, that is all that we are, and that is all that we shall stay...

Chapter 10

Sitting in my office, I tapped on my computer, starting at a financial report. My eyes were going crossed as I've worked for over ten hours and it was well past 7 pm. Most of my coworkers had gone home, and I was alone at the office still working.

I guess this was the consequence of me playing hooky yesterday with Hannah. It was well worth it. I loved her sleeping over. I still can't get the imagine of her sleeping in my jersey out of my mind.

Not to mention the anal sex. Fuck me. I love how Hannah is down to do literally anything. She's such a wild card and I love that about her. Between giving me road head, fucking in the public parking garage, and anal sex, it felt like I was hooking up with a porn star.

It was great that she connected with me on so many levels. Not only was it sexual, but personality wise too. We held a lot of the same values, and I haven't had a friend like this in a while.

Friend...that word. Why was it triggering to me. I wanted to be more.

I sighed.

Perhaps it's for the best we weren't friends. None of my serious relationships ever worked out. If Hannah and I were something more, we were doomed to follow that same path as my other exes, and honestly I don't want that. I barely ever speak to any of my exes, and I would hate to lose Hannah to that fate.

I sighed once more, smashing the down arrow on my keyboard as my eyes scanned the financial document. At this point all I wanted to do was go home, but of course this client wanted their shit done by the end of the week.

In the middle of the review, my phone rang and I looked down to see it was Hannah calling me.

I smirked and answered it, "Sup."

"Hi, can you talk? She asked.

"I'm at work..."

"Oh, shit, sorry."

"No, it's cool. I'm pretty much by myself right now. Everyone left for the day except for a few people at work."

"Oh, damn, I was hoping you were off. You could swing by and keep me some company. It's so damn slow today. It's just a couple of barflies and that's it."

"Oh, I'm sorry. I would if could, but someone made me play hooky yesterday."

"Sorry! But don't lie, yesterday was hot, wasn't it?"

"Yeah it was." Memories of the prior night replied in my mind. The thought of my dick being inside Hannah's ass made my insides twitch.

"I'm touching myself right now thinking of how you made me come."

"What? In front of everyone?"

"No, I'm in the storeroom. I told my coworker I was getting supplies, but really I wanted to have phone sex with you. You can whisper sweet nothings in my ear while I finger myself and you can jerk off listening to me moan."

"Hannah, I'm at work."

"So am I, aren't you in an office or something? Just close the door."

I bit my lip, and stood up from my chair. Poking my head out of my office door, I scanned the open office floor covered in cubicles and noted there wasn't any one around. The only person on my floor was another account manager whose door was closed.

I knew I shouldn't masturbate at my job, but Hannah was driving me towards that sin. I couldn't explain it but when I'm with her all reasoning goes out the window. Just the thought of her fingering herself was making me hard, and my cock was tenting in my slacks.

"Fuck it..." I muttered, closing my office door.

I sat back in my chair, and unzipped my pants and started rubbing my swollen length.

"My pants are down now. I'm touching myself." I whispered.

"Good, so am I. Fuck am I horny. I'm so fucking wet..." she moaned.

"Yeah? What are you wearing right now?"

"Just a leather mini skirt, and tank top."

"Fuck me...that sounds sexy. Is your skirt hiked up right now?"

"Of course it is. I've pushed my thong to the side, and I'm fingering myself right now."

"Fuck..." I groaned, as my hand shifted faster.

"I'm thinking about your black cock going inside me. You're so fucking big..." she moaned.

"Yeah?"

"Yes, baby. I love the way you stretch me out. It feels so fucking good. My body is trembling imagining your black python."

"Black python?" I smirked.

"Yeah...that's what I'm calling him. Because he's long, and thick and when it has you, it doesn't let go until you pop."

"I like that..."

She giggled. "What about you, what are you wearing?"

"I'm in my office attire. White shirt, tie, and a pair of black slacks."

"Fuck me that's hot."

"Right now, I'm sitting in my office chair, in front of my desk. My pants are opened slightly, and my cock is out. I'm jerking off right now, thinking of you. I'm thinking of you coming to my office and riding my hard cock."

"Oh, I'd like that. We could push the stuff off your desk and you can take me then and there. I could put my legs on your shoulders and you can make me come. I'll be so fucking loud that every one in the building could hear."

"Fuck..." I groaned, feeling it.

"Yes, baby. I'm so drenched thinking about it." Hannah shrieked over the phone and exhaled loudly.

"I'm hard too..." my legs quivered just thinking about the erotic imagine of us together.

My phone buzzed and I saw it was my mom.

"Shit..." I muttered.

"What is it?" She asked. "Did someone walk in on you?"

"Nah, it's my ma. I gotta take this. I only check up on her once a week. I'm sorry to cut out early."

"It's cool. I know how much you love her. Plus, I'm a single mom. I hope Thomas is as sweet as you when he grows up."

"He will be. You're a good mom."

"Aww, thanks Deshawn. I'll talk you you later. Perhaps we can hang out again before the orgy?"

"Yeah, I'll like that. Bye."

"Bye."

I hung up the phone, and quickly pulled up my pants, attempting to control myself after the sexy conversation I just had with Hannah. By the time I was ready, my mom's call dropped, so I had to call her back.

"Hello?" My mom answered.

"Sorry about that, ma, I was busy at work, and didn't see your call until it was too late." I lied.

"Oh, that's okay. I know your busy at work. If now's a bad time..."

"No, no, no. It's good. I need a break. I've been working for over ten hours."

"Deshawn, your not overworking yourself are you. It's not healthy how much time you put in the office."

"Well, ma if I want to keep making the six figures I make, you gotta put in the work."

"I guess so…" she sighed.

"I just wish you had more of a social life. It seems like all you do is work and go home."

"Well, I shoot hoops when I can. I got my gang of buddies that go the gym all the time."

"Yeah, but I guess what I'm saying is, I wish you would find a woman. You know, you're getting older."

"Ma, I'm only 25. I got plenty of time to find someone."

"Yeah, but I'm getting older. Mary down the block just had her first grandbaby and she's a few years younger than me."

"So you'd want me to have a kid?"

"No, no, I'm not telling you to go out there and knock a whole bunch of women up, I guess what I'm saying is I'm lonely. I would love to have a son or daughter to babysit for a weekend, or something. I don't know."

"Ah, I got you."

"Yeah, I'm sorry, I know you are young and single living the bachelor life in Washington."

"No, no. I'm actually seeing someone."

"Really? Who is she?"

"Hannah, she's a white girl, with tattoos and piercings. She has red hair and a gorgeous smile you could just get lost in."

"Really? She sounds beautiful, but I didn't think that would be your type. You've usually dated more conservatively."

"I know, but she's amazing. Down to earth, and adventurous. She's really opening me up." I grinned. In more ways than one, I thought to myself, but I didn't want to fill my mom in all the dirty deeds we've done.

"She sounds sweet."

"She is."

"So you're dating her?"

"No, she's actually been wanting us to be friends. We're just fooling around,"

"Oh... you wrapping it up?"

"Ma..."

"Fooling around can lead to a lot of things..."

"Didn't you just say you wanted grandbabies?"

"Yes, from your married wife. Not some side chick."

"Ma, Hannah is more than just a booty call. Our friendships is deep. I know it's only been a couple of weeks since I met her, but she's becoming a really good friend. I like hanging out with her."

"Oh, then why the hesitation from her?"

"I think a part of the reason why is because she's a single mother, and she's afraid that if we dated things could get complicated."

"She's right. I was very selective of the men I brought around you. Especially at a young age. How old is her boy?"

"Five."

"Yeah, boys his age tend to latch on easy. Just be careful with her..."

"Ma what is that supposed to mean?"

"I'm not telling you not to pursue her, just know that she's a package deal. When you date her, you get her and her son. You haven't had much luck dating and if this one fizzles out...not only would you be breaking up with her, you'd be breaking up with her son."

"I know Ma...I know, it's just..." I closed my eyes and breathed. "I just haven't felt this way about someone in a while."

"I gotcha. I love you. I just don't want to see you try hurt. You are all I have in this world."

"I know, Ma. You'll always be my number one."

"You're too sweet baby, but it sounds like I might be having some competition for that number one spot."

"Too soon, Ma."

"I don't know, it sounds like you are swooning for her."

"I don't know." I sighed, feeling like I was being pulled in different directions. "She's been on my mind though."

"I know the feeling. Just be safe okay?"

"I will. I love you. I'm free next weekend you'd want me to swing by Norfolk to say hello?"

"Next weekend might be bad because my walking group is doing a race in Richmond, but three weeks from now I'm free, did you want to do something then?"

"Yeah, that would be fun. Okay, I gotta get back to work. Talk you to later."

"Of course. Bye, baby."

"Bye, ma."

I hung up the phone and sighed. My mom was right about Hannah, dating her would put me closer to Thomas, but I couldn't resist. There was a force pulling me towards her. With Hannah it was more than just sex. There was something more, and I'd be a damn fool if I didn't explore more of it.

Chapter 11

Walking up to the mansion in the expensive neighborhood in McLean, I felt out of place. Between the gate house and the long driveway, this usually wasn't my scene. The large three story white brick mansion in front of me, with the large bay windows and black shutters screamed that it belonged to a rich politician, and the last thing I wanted to be involved in was some tabloid article about how a filthy rich congressman spent his nights fulfilling his sexual fantasies.

Looking over at Hannah, she didn't look nearly as nervous as me. She strolled confidently down the driveway, making her way past the multiple cars parked on the paved street.

She did look amazing. Behind the setting afternoon sun, she glowed in her sexy low cut minidress, that showed off her curves. Her ass cheeks were nearly hanging out, as they jiggled with each step, and with her exposed cleavage, I joyfully watched her tatted tits bounce. Her red hair was down, and she wore a lot of makeup and hoop earrings. Honestly, she looked like a mixture of a hooker and pornstar, but regardless she looked sexy as hell.

Me on the other hand, I felt like bum. Honestly, as a guy what do you wear to an orgy that was sexy? I ended up picking out a pair of tight grey slacks and a silk blue shirt, that was opened by two buttons. Hannah said I looked sexy, but I have my doubts. It's hard to good, when your standing next to a goddess like her.

Approaching the large home, I could see the lights turned on, and could hear loud music coming from the large black door.

Hannah pressed the doorbell, and I could hear it ring throughout the house.

"Coming!" A voice called out.

Hannah looked at me and smiled, "are you okay?"

"Yeah, just anxious..."

"You'd be fine. Just stick by me."

"Okay."

I heard footsteps and the door opened to an older white man. He looked to be Italian, in his sixties, and was wearing robe. He had a large beer gut, slicked back black hair, and more chest hair than I care to admit. In his hand was a lit cigar and a glass of liquor.

"Ah, Hannah...it's good to see you." His accent was thick, and sounded like he was from New Jersey. Perhaps he was in the mafia judging by his golden chain and multiple rings on his fingers.

"It's good to see too, Tony." Hannah opened her arms wide and gave the big man a hug and he laughed, hugging her back. During their hug, his hands lowered from from her back, and squeezed and smacked her ass. He then winked at me.

"Hey!" Hannah laughed slapping his shoulder. "That hurt!"

"Sorry, Hannah, I couldn't resist. An ass like that can't be ignored. My man knows what I'm talking about." He chuckled, placing his cigar in his mouth.

I gave him a polite smile, and nodded as I picked up several #metoo vibes from him.

"Is this, Deshawn?" He pointed towards me.

"Yeah," Hannah answered.

"Nice to finally meet you! Hannah has talked a lot about you."

"About me?" I questioned.

"Yeah, you see, Hannah, and I are close. This orgy group is a tight knit group. We share a lot with each other. She tells me you two are fucking around."

"Yeah...something like that."

"Consider yourself lucky. A pussy like hers is one in a million."

"Tony!" Hannah laughed and slapped his shoulder. "And what about your wife's?"

"Shit, Hannah, my wife has tasted and fucked that pussy of yours, and she could confirm it too. One in a million."

Hannah rolled her eyes as she blushed.

"Are you going to invite us in or are you going to keep shouting to the neighbors about my cunt?" She smiled.

"They could only wish..." he laughed boastfully before sitting his cigar into his mouth. "Come, come, everyone is already here."

Tony stepped back and allowed us to enter his grand home. My jaw dropped at the grandeur of the place. Between the marble floors and large chandelier at the entrance, the house screamed millionaire.

"Nice place?" I commented, looking at the expensive fixtures.

"You think so? I prefer my beach house in the Miami, but this is okay. Serves me well, when I'm working in DC."

"Politician?" I asked.

"Lobbyist. There's no money in politics. Trust me."

I nodded, as his flashy wealth finally made sense.

"So Deshawn have you ever been a part of an orgy before?" He asked.

"No, this is my first one."

"Okay, just a couple of ground rules. Like you and Hannah, we have two other singles here. The other four, including me are married, so keep that in mind. What you do in the room is free game, anything outside that room needs to be discussed with the other partner."

"Fair enough."

"Good; second one is a biggy. Condoms are worn for any intercourse. If you're giving or taking oral, or taking a handjob, you didn't need a condom, but any time your dick gets into a pussy, it better be wrapped."

"Got it."

"Good, and don't wear the same condom for every woman. We have shit ton of condoms in there. Just change it out whenever you switch to a new woman."

"Okay."

"Good, last thing, don't do anything no one is uncomfortable with. If she says she doesn't want it in the ass, don't pin her down and shove it in her ass. If you don't want to have sex with a particular person or don't want to be kissed or something, speak up. We respect everyone's boundaries, got it?"

"Yes, sir."

"I have a feeling I'll like you. Come, everyone's already stared."

"You serious?" Hannah groaned.

"Yeah, we were going to wait for you, but everyone is usually horny when they arrive. Somebody kisses someone and next thing you know, we're fucking. I was just about to get my own dick wet when you rang."

I looked at Tony and smirked.

"So whose here," Hannah asked.

"My wife Vicki, plus our neighbors down the block, that rap star, Big John, and his wife, Mercedes."

"Oh, I love Big John." Hannah gushed.

I rose my eyebrow at her.

"So does my wife..." Tony chuckled, letting out a puff of his cigar. "Every lady loves Big John."

"We also got two new faces, not including your guy."

"Who? Eric and Dana could make it?"

"Nah, Eric has a business trip in Vegas. Brought Dana with him so naturally those two are probably fucking in some desert orgy out there. Damn does Vegas throw the best fucking sex parties."

"So whose here then?" Hannah asked.

"Two ringers we picked up from online. Tyrese, big black guy, used to play college football, then some skinny little Asian chick named Kelly. I think shes Korean or something. She was pretty shy. It took her a while to warm up to everyone. Part of me thought she was going to walk out."

"Oh, did you dazzle her with that Tony charm."

"Nah, my wife did. The Asian chick is bi. All my wife had to do was make out with her and eat her pussy. Next thing you know; the party was on."

He led us down the hall, towards a back room. The closer we got to the room, the louder the music from outside became. Opening the door, my eyes opened wide to the multiple men and woman having sex. In total there were five people. Three women and two men, each twisted around each other, moaning and groaning while they fucked each other.

The room itself looked to be designed for this type of dubious behavior, as the room had several sofas and cushions spread out for various positions. The room was windowless, but had multiple mirrors in the walls and ceilings allowing you to watch yourself while you fucked. In the corner of the room was a stereo, playing a techno like remix, and on the opposite end of the room was a marble mini bar with multiple liquor bottles, wines and beers, along with glasses. In the center of the room was a small wooden table with a large glass jar filled with condoms.

Tony whistled, and yelled, "hey, listen up, Hannah is here!"

The crowd stopped what they were doing and waved at us.

"Hey guys!" Hannah waved, walking over towards the bar. "Deshawn you want a shot of tequila?"

"Yeah, I need it." I chuckled, admiring all of the naked women in front of me.

Tony pointed at me and said, "this here is Deshawn, her friend. I've already filled him in on the ground rules."

"Hi!" The crowd greeted, before resuming their sexual activities before we walked in. Once more I heard different moans and groans, and the sound of skin clapping together. While Hannah stood at the bar preparing our drinks, Tony placed his hand behind me and got close. He was a little too close for someone I just met as I could smell his aftershave, but considering we probably were both going to be naked in a few minutes, I couldn't complain.

Beside me, he pointed towards a fifty year old curvy blonde with a pudgy belly, with a flat pale ass and saggy tits. She was wearing black stockings, attached to a garter belt.

"Over there is my wife, Vicki…"

I'm not going to lie, I expected Tony to be married to some trophy wife half his age with fake tits, but it looked like he at least was married to someone close to his age. Vicki was on all fours, being railed by a large black man. The black man looked like an offensive lineman for a football team, as he was large and big. Like giant big. He had a large belly, and a muscular chest, with a short low cut fade. The long gold chain around his neck bounced every time he pounded his dick into Vicki.

"That is…"

"Big John…" I guessed.

"Yeah. You listen to his music,"

"Yeah, he's a good rapper."

"Never been one for rap. Prefer classic rock, but his stuff ain't half bad."

"Yeah, it's weird that I'm sharing a room with a celebrity."

"About that…" Tony paused and rubbed the back of his head. "There's another rule I forgot to mention. Everything that happens in this room stays in this room."

"Of course."

"No, I'm being serious. Me, I really don't care who you tell. Every politician knows my sexual preferences, and every politician knows that I have enough dirt on them to make their own mothers disown them. Big John over there though…"

I turned my attention to the ape of a human being. Sweat rolled down his brow, as he gripped Vicki's ass cheeks shoving every inch he had into her.

"He has a rep to protect. He can't have everyone knowing he's a part of a sex club. It would be a PR nightmare. More than likely he's going to have to sign a NDA after all of this."

"That's cool. I got a high paying job too. I can't afford to get fired from it, as I don't think my bosses would like to know how I spend my weekends."

"What do you do?"

"I'm a financial advisor."

"Ah, you run portfolios?"

"Yeah..."

"You and I should talk after this. I wouldn't mind throwing a couple million your way to manage."

"You serious? You barely even met me? What if lose it all?"

He chuckled, "then it's a risk I'm willing to take. Listen, you're your brave enough to strip naked and bare all in front of complete strangers, I think you're wise enough to handle a couple million. If you do good, I'll throw some more money at you."

"Wow, thanks."

Tony nodded, "that's beside the point. Let's not talk business let's talk pussy. Over there, getting eaten out by Vicki is Kelly."

I stared at the skinny Asian with beige skin. She was beautiful with almond shaped eyes and flawless skin. Her jet black hair was matted on the floor as she laid on her backside with her legs hoisted in the air in a wide V allowing Vicki to have access to her. Kelly had small perky tits, small brown nipples, and a small shaved strip of black pubic hair above her brown colored snatch.

Vicki's face was buried into Kelly's folds, slurping up her insides, while, Big John squatted behind Vicki, fucking her hard. All three members of the threesome moaned, as they enjoyed their pleasures. Kelly squealed, rubbing her taut nipples, and lifted her legs higher, allowing Vicki greater access to her center.

"Like I said, she's a little wallflower when she first got here, a bit timid."

"Why is that? I would've thought she would've been down for this. Especially since she reached out to you."

Tony shrugged. "It's a lot to take in at first. I mean, most people are used to having sex with only one person in an intimate private setting. Here, everything is exposed. You are naked with five other individuals. It's a lot for a first timer. It's your first time too, I'd imagine you'd be nervous."

"Yeah, a bit."

Tony nodded, "you'll be fine. Just remember the objective here is to get off."

I nodded, and Hannah returned with three shot glasses in her hand.

"Tony I made you one, so you would feel left out."

"Ah, that's my girl." He took the shot glass from her, and I took one too. Tony held his high and said, "to getting your dick wet."

"To getting your dick wet..." Hannah and I both replied, giggling. We took the shot of the clear tequila and it was a sharp smooth taste that tickled my throat.

"Another?" She asked.

"Yeah, one more." I replied.

"None, for me, sweetie. You keep this up and you'd be fucking a limp dick."

Hannah laughed, " Tony, I know you'll always get hard for this ass."

"You know I would sweetie." He winked.

Hannah laughed once more and walked back to the bar to get another round of shots for us.

"So where was I..." Tony muttered, looking at the crowd having sex in front of us.

"Ah. So, over there we have the sexy,, Mercedes ..." Tony pointed at a woman, no older than thirty light skinned sista. The black woman had a hourglass model type body with large tits, which I'm eighty percent sure are fake, along with a plump ass. She was riding a black man hard in the reverse cowgirl position. As she bounced on his pole, the black man growled, slapping her ass.

"That is Big John's wife. She gives amazing blowjobs, and her dick riding skills..." Tony groaned, closing his eyes. "She I'll leave you drained for days."

I smirked, "watching Mercedes move with grace like a stripper on the black man's dick.

"Last but not least, we have Tyrese." Tony pointed to the muscular black man, laying in his back as Mercedes rode him. "He's our other ringer for the night. Unlike Kelly, this isn't Tyrese's first orgy. He's been to others in the area. We actually met him up at one in Baltimore."

"Oh, okay.."

Tyrese looked up to me and gave me the casual *sup* nod. I returned the gesture and then turned to see, Hannah, carrying two more shots.

"Ok. Let's do this and then get our fuck on." Hannah replied, handing me the glass.

"It's about time. I was getting blue balls over here." Tony muttered, dropping his robe. I smirked, and held in a laugh, looking at Tony's fat hairy ass as he walked towards the glass jar of condoms. He didn't have the biggest cock as it dangled between us legs, but his lack of inches m didn't seem to bother him as he held his head up high.

Hannah and I cheers our glass and down the clear liquid. Once we were done, Hannah and I placed our glasses on a nearby table and we both got naked ourselves.

I was already hard, watching and listening to all the sex going on around me, but upon seeing Hannah's naked curves, my cock felt like concrete.

"Ah, I see someone ready to play." Hannah smirked, coming close to kiss me. As our lips touched, she jerked my cock with vigor.

I groaned, kissing her neck as Tony approached us.

"Got room for one more?" He asked.

"Always…" she smirked, turning to kiss him. Her hand left my cock and went to his as she jerked his softness. He groaned, licking her neck.

It was strange at first to see Hannah with another man. However, the more I watched, the more I got turned on. I loved watching Hannah, pleasure Tony. From the way she moaned, and looked at him, all the way to how she kissed him. Each moment of them together was pleasing to the eyes.

My cock jutted out, and Hannah used both hands to jerk Tony and me off simultaneously. She then bend down and rotated between sucking both of us off.

I groaned and placed my hands on my back, enjoying the tantalizing feeling of Hannah's tongue wrapped around me.

"Damn Hannah…" Tony groaned, reaching down to massage her tit. "Hey, Deshawn…"

"Yeah?" I answered.

"Here…" he handed me a condom. "I'm still softer than a wet noddle right now. You can have first dibs."

"Thanks," I smirked.

"How did you want me?" Hannah asked, looking up at me.

"On your back, with your legs up in the air. I got your pussy, Tony gets your mouth."

"Hannah, I knew I liked this guy." Tony chuckled.

"I told you." She winked at Tony, and the assumed the position with her legs spread in a wide V. Tony squatted over her face, and Hannah began sucking his cock, while I wrapped my cock with a condom.

Once covered, I slipped into Hannah and groaned. She was wet. It was a different experience fucking Hannah with another man. For one I couldn't see her expressions, while I knew she liked it based off of the way she twitched and moan, I just couldn't see her emotions. Instead

I was greeted to an image of Tony's sweaty hairy ass, as he dipped his cock into Hannah's mouth as she gobbled his load.

It made no difference on the view, her pussy still felt the same. It was still felt amazing. It still made my cock twitch and made me want to be buried in it. My hands slid down her curvy sides down to thick thighs, and plump calves. I held her legs upright, shoving every inch I had to her. Hannah's toes pointed to the ceiling, while her moans were muffled by the sound of Tony's cock suffocating her.

I didn't know what was wrong with me. Most people would be disgusted at hearing another woman choke while deep throating a man, but I wasn't. The sound was intoxicating. It made the sex with her even more thrilling.

I was in the zone, taking Hannah when another woman strolled up to me. I couldn't see who it was as my focus was on Hannah. The woman bent down beside me, and I watched her red painted finger nails rub my chest.

"Hi..." she whispered in my ear.

I turned to find Vicki squatting beside me. She gave me a naughty smile, before touching my chin.

"You're cute." She complimented.

"And you're sexy. I love your mature curves...."

"Have you ever been with an older woman?" She asked.

"No, but I get feeling I'm about too..."

She laughed, and breathed deeply, "you got a nice body. So young and firm." She slapped my ass and I couldn't help but to smile.

"Thanks, I love your saggy tits."

"Really?" She asked, perking her chest up. "Most men your age would be revolted by this body."

"Nah, those tits good enough to suck."

"Did you want to taste them,"

"Yes, ma'am."

Vicki leaned closer to me, and I angled my head suck on her nipple. Her soft skin tasted like roses, as my tongue twirled around her supple tissue. Her skin felt like a warm cotton blanket, as I nuzzled my face in her breasts. She giggled and brought my chin towards her mouth.

Seconds later, her tongue met my own in an erotic kiss. I groaned making out with Vicki as I continued to pump into Hannah. Vicki's hands were all over me as she explored every detail on my body. She rubbed my six pack, and her hands slid down my ass. I groaned when her hands grabbed my balls, and I twitched when she rolled them in her hands.

"Fuck…" I muttered.

"I brought a condom with me. How'd you like to fuck me?"

"I'd love too…" I grinned.

I pulled out of Hannah and tossed the used condom off to the side. Tony didn't waste any time taking my place with Hannah. As soon as I was out of her, he climbed on top of her, resuming to pound her hard. I smirked, watching Hannah get it, before my attention was pulled back to Vicki.

"Don't worry, my husband has her in good hands. For right now you are all mine."

"Yes ma'am." I grinned.

Vicki giggled and unwrapped the condom, and rolled the latex down my hard shaft. She jerked me off slowly and whispered in my ear.

"You got a nice big cock."

"Thanks."

"I love black cock. Did you know that?"

"I do now." I grinned.

"I have a challenge for you. Can you make me come?"

"Yeah, I think I can. Get on all fours."

She snickered and assumed the doggy position. I groaned looking at her chubby ass and smacked it once before slipping in her ass. She was a bit looser than Hannah, but she still felt good.

"Fuck me... you feel good..." she uttered.

"So do you..." I bit my lip, as I slid in and out of her. My body tingled from the erotic thrill of fucking someone new. I liked having sex with Vicki. Through she was older, she knew how to work my cock. It wasn't just me pumping into her, she rocked her own body back and forth, and she like to twerk her ass on my dick, giving me a little sexy show.

I groaned and slapped her ass twice, mesmerized by the shape of her body. With her, my senses were on fire, my cock burned from the wetness of her cunt. My eyes were delighted to see the jiggle of her fat ass and the sway of her plump tits. I could smell her musk, as her white juices painted my condom. Her moans only drove me to go harder and faster. My fingers dug into her soft flesh, turning her pale skin red where my fingers were. Goddamn did I love taking the mature.

I heard a familiar moan and looked up to see Hannah in the same position as Vicki. Face down, ass up, Tony plowed into her, grunting like an ape as his face turned red. Sweat rolled down his forehead as he gave it to her hard and fast.

He noticed me staring and winked. "How do you like fucking my wife?"

"She's good. I love this pussy."

"Why do you think I married it?" He laughed.

"A little less talking and more fucking please. I'm almost there..." Vicki moaned.

"Oh, you. I'm just trying to get closer to our host." Tony laughed. "Deshawn do me a favor, smack that woman's ass.

"With pleasure..." I tapped her rear several times and Vicki shrieked.

"Oh, fuck me. That's it. Take it. Fucking take it. Yeah, yeah, yeah. Fuck me! Oh God!" She squealed. The next few words were inaudible. I didn't know what she said. I didn't care. She was all mine.

I growled and pushed her flat on the ground. I pumped into her hard and fast at a blistering pace. Sweat covered my brow and dripped from my forehead onto her back. I moved at a violent pace, and knew I couldn't last long at this speed. I didn't know what took over me, I was possessed. I was a monster as I tore that mature pussy up. Even when she came, I still keep going, pumping into her filling up her body until I was limp.

When I was through, I pulled out her, watching as she laid shivering.

"Goddamn, Deshawn. Left her numb." Tony grinned.

Vicki placed one hand on her forehead gasping for air. With the other hand she beckoned me closer.

I leaned close and she kissed me. "That was one hell of a dick you got there. Hannah, what ever you do. Don't let this man out of your life."

While Hannah was getting railed she looked at me and smiled. I couldn't explain it then, but I never felt closer to anyone in that moment than I did with Hannah.

Chapter 12

Sitting at the bar, I watched as Hannah was being triple teamed by Big John, Tyrese, and Tony. I couldn't explain why watching Hannah get pumped by three dicks turned me on, but it did.

I could see why men like cuckolding their wives and girlfriends. It was a different form of pleasure. Almost like you are living vicariously through them. Listening to her moan, and watching her face fill with pleasure, I knew she was in her right place. This was home to her, and I was happy for her.

It had been an hour into the orgy, and I'd already came twice, and needed a breather from the strenuous activity. Never before had I sexually exhausted myself like this before. It felt like doing wind sprints after practice, the only difference was the wind sprints felt amazing and made you come.

"Are you almost done with your drink?" Mercedes asked me.

"Almost, why?" I smirked.

"Well, you are the only man not fucking. Vicki, Kelly and I want a dick to join us. You're up. Are you hard?"

"I'm a bit soft."

"We'll, get you there. Come here..." she grabbed my hand and led me towards an open area where, Vicki and Kelly stood. Both women were making out when I joined them.

"Ladies, look who I found, staring at Hannah."

"Yes! Another dick!" Kelly giggled.

I smirked at the thin Asian as she longer seemed like the shy wallflower that Tony described her as. It seemed like she had blossomed into a full fledged sex addict like the rest of us.

"Ah, he's in love, girls. Leave him be." Vicki smiled.

"No, we're just friends." I replied.

"Sure…" she winked.

"Just friends, huh?" Kelly asked, arching an eyebrow. "So if y'all are friends, she wouldn't mind if I do this?" She grabbed my chin and kissed me. I groaned, feeling her tongue slide past mine and I held her waist bringing her closer to me. As we made out, I felt Vicki and Mercedes circle around me.

"Hey, don't hog him. He's the only dick we have." Mercedes' hand wrapped around my cock and gently stroked me, while, Vicki sensually rubbed my back and stomach.

Feeling all three woman touch me, I felt like I was in heaven. It was the foursome that every guy dreamed off.

Pushing Kelly, away, I looked into her eyes and said, "you and Vicki make out."

"Anything, you say." Kelly smirked and moved towards Vicki to kiss her. I watched as the two made out, and saw Mercedes drop below my vision to her knees. I then felt her mouth take me as she sucked my cock.

Between the stimulation of Mercedes' blowjob, and the make out session between Vicki and Kelly, I was hard again.

"Oh, ladies, we got a hard dick alert." Mercedes giggled, stroking my stiffness.

They cheered and Vicki walked away from Kelly to grab a condom. While Vicki was away, Kelly joined Mercedes on her knees giving me a sensual double blowjob. Watching both sexy Black and Asian women lick and spit on my cock was amazing. I felt like I was staring in my own porno watching the two women work my pole. My dick was was dripping wet by the time Vicki rolled the latex down my shaft. She gave it a few good tugs before backing away and saying, "Mercedes , you get first fuck."

"Don't mind if I do." She pushed be back into the sofa, and I sat down watching as she turned around for me to see her plump round ass.

She was so damn thick. She sat on my cock in reverse cowgirl position, and then posted her legs on my thighs allowing her to bounce in my cock with vigor. Leaning back on the couch, I held her body, watching as she worked my cock. She moaned, sliding up and down every inch, while, Vicki and Kelly squatted in front of her, sucking my balls and licking her cunt. Both woman provided added pleasure to our already in growing one.

I groaned and squeezed Mercedes's fat fake tit. My thumb brushed over her taut brown nipple and she shivered. In the distance, I heard other moans, and looked across the room to see Hannah being pumped by Big Joe while jerking off the other guys. Watching her take all of those dicks made me even harder. I couldn't explain why but I was getting off by the sexual visual. It was sensory overload between the sexy image of Hannah, the feeling of Mercedes's tit in my hand, the tightness of her pussy, and the tongues of Kelly and Vicki around my balls.

I gasped as my lungs extorted themselves. Sweat rolled down my forehead, my hands shook from the surge of pleasure coursing through me. I was on fire and all I wanted was more.

"Ugh, how does that pussy feel?" Mercedes moaned.

"Good..."

"You like the way I ride it?"

"Yeah, it's sexy as hell..." I groaned. She leaned her head back and her relaxed hair tickled my skin. For most guys, they would've been all about Mercedes . I mean she was a thick ebony, what more could you want? But what Hannah was doing in the distance kept me busy. Despite the sexy three women circling me, my eyes were solely on Hannah. I smiled, watching her get tripled plugged with a dick in the ass, her pussy and mouth. She could barely move as she was penetrated by the multiple cocks. Her pale tatted skin had a moist sheen of sweat, and her red hair was in disarray. Call me crazy, but I couldn't think she could be sexier. What in the hell was wrong with me? A million guys would kill to be in the position I was in. Cock deep in pussy with his balls being sucked and licked by two beautiful women, yet all I wanted to get off on was the fact that Hannah is getting railed by three men.

Kelly tapped Mercedes's shoulder and held a condom in her hand.

"'My turn to ride that black stallion."

Mercedes laughed, "he's all yours." She rolled off me leaving me sitting in the chair with my hard dick upright.

Kelly jerked me off, before tossing the used condom and replacing it with a new one.

"Where did you want me?" I asked.

"I want to be on my back."

"You got it."

Kelly laid down on the couch, with her head on the armrest. Hovering above her, I rubbed my cock before slipping inside her. Placing her leg on my shoulder, I pounded into her. She moaned, grabbing the seat cushion behind her.

"Yeah, yeah, yeah, take it. Fucking take it!" She yelled.

I squeezed her breasts and licked her smooth shaven beige skinned leg as I continued to ram into her.

Once again I was distracted by the moans of Hannah. I didn't know what was with me. It was hard to stay focused as all wanted to do was watch her receive pleasure. My eyes were on Hannah until Vicki blocked my view.

"Hi…"

"You know you can go over there and watch."

"No, I'm good."

"You sure? Us ladies can handle ourselves if you want."

"No, no, no, I'm good."

"Okay, you just seem distracted."

"Sorry, it's just a lot."

"I understand." She smirked. "Perhaps this will focus you." Vicki sat on Kelly's face and on cue, Kelly began to eat out Vicki. She moaned, rolling her hips, allowing Kelly to lick different crevices of her center. Vicki then grabbed my chin and kissed me. I moaned , feeling her tongue on mine.

As I kissed Vicki, I heard another yelp, and I turned to see that Mercedes had joined Hannah, creating a sexy fivesome. She was massaging Hannah, adding another layer to her pleasure. Hannah's body shook and she screamed as she came. Even though she was experiencing her orgasm, the men didn't stop. They kept pleasuring her. Upon seeing that, my body felt its own orgasm coming. It wasn't Kelly's pussy that did it. Nor was it Vicki's kiss. Instead it was Hannah that got me to blow. That strange cuckhold was rocket fuel for my orgasm as I filled the condom with my seed.

When I was through, I pulled out of Kelly and she kissed me.

"That was good. Come find me when your hard again. I want to ride that cock."

"Sure." I gasped, sitting down in the couch. Kelly left to go get a drink while Vicki sat next to me. We both continued to watch Hannah have sex.

"Having a good time," she asked.

"Yeah, " my eyes didn't leave Hannah's as she passionately moaned.

"Good. How long have you like her?"

"What?" I gawked, looking back at Vicki.

"Ah, that got your attention. Not the two smoking chicks you were fucking, but the question of if you like someone or not."

"Hannah and I are just friends."

"Bullshit."

"No, seriously we are."

"You don't look at someone like that as friends. You got a cuckhold eye."

"What?"

"It's what my husband gives me when I'm taking dick that's not his. You get off from her pleasure."

"No, it's just sexy."

"Call it you want, you have eyes for her."

"It's not..."

"You'd be good together. Hannah needs a man in her life. Her ex was no good, but you...I can't tell you got a good head on your shoulders."

"Thanks..."

"Have you told her how you felt?"

"There's nothing to tell..."

"There's something. Trust me. You need to tell her. Girls like Hannah are a rare. You better take her before someone else does." She winked. "Now come on, I'm getting drier than the desert over here." She leaned back and held her legs out. "You might not be hard, but I'm still horny. Get to licking."

"Yes, ma'am." I replied, burying myself into her folds.

Chapter 13

What Vicki and my ma said, continue to repeat in my head. These feelings I had for Hannah, they weren't going away. They only intensified. Like an echo in my mind. I kept hearing what they said about telling her the truth. Those words, repeated in my mind every second of the day. It infected me to my core. I felt like a damn ready to explode and I knew I had to tell her. I had to tell her how I felt.

It was all I could think of while I had sex with Hannah. I should be turned on, fucking her in the backroom of her dive bar, but I'm not. I should be focusing on the way her pussy feels around my cock, and how her tits jiggles every time I pump my cock into her, but I'm not. No, instead I keep thinking about us. I keep thinking about how to express my feelings about her.

Hannah gripped the upper bar of the storage cabinet and moaned. Her body moved with mine, as I held her ass, fucking her hard and fast. Her leather mini skirt was hiked up, and her spaghetti top straps were pushed down off her shoulders, allowing me to glimpse at her tatted breasts. My pants were unzipped, and my hard cock, protruded out, slipping in and out of her wet cunt. Her curvy legs were wrapped around my ass, as I took her in the upright position. Sweat rolled down both our bodies as we were twisted in an erotic pretzel. Boxes of supplies fell to the floor, as Hannah reached up to adjust her position.

Driven by lust and sin, we were loud, but we didn't care. When the moment hits, it hits. I had to have her. She had to have me. The only people on the bar were the usuals, and we both knew they weren't going to say shit. Besides, they probably were turned on listening to our grunts and moans.

"Oh yeah, right there…right there…" Hannah gasped, clutching the wooden frame above her and her body twisted in my hands. Her insides convulsed and I felt a rush of my own.

"Fuck…" I groaned, emptying myself into the condom. Once again, this woman knew how to drain every single drop from me. I pulled out of her and placed her down on the floor. Both of us looked like hot messes while we shuffled about. While Hannah pushed down her skirt, and placed the straps of her top back on her shoulders, I removed the condom, tossing it in the trash and pulled my pants up.

"That was good."

"Yeah, it was."

"We're always good together aren't we?" She grinned, looking at a near by mirror, combing her fingers through her red hair to get rid of the sex hairdo I gave her.

"Yeah, we are…" I mumbled.

Hannah, grabbed her purse nearby and pulled out a stick of lipgloss. She looked at me through the mirror, as she applied the makeup.

"Hey are you okay? You seemed out of it."

"Yeah, I'm good."

"You sure? I mean that was some of the craziest sex I've had, and you act like it was average."

"Nah, it was good. Trust me. It was good." I chuckled, rubbing the back of my head.

"Then what is it?"

Realizing that she was going to keep digging until I confessed I sighed and replied, "it's about us."

"What about?" She turned from the mirror and looks into my eyes. "You want to stop fucking or something?"

"No, no…far from that. It's just…" I closed my eyes, trying to find the right words to tell her. "I caught feelings for you, Hannah."

Her eyes opened wide and she didn't reply. I didn't know if she was mad or surprised, but I continued.

"I know we were only supposed to stay as friends, but I can't stay that way anymore. I can't keep living this lie that I don't have feelings for you. That I don't want to be with you. I know you have your reservations on dating, but I don't. I'm ready for that step. I'm ready to be with you. I want you." I reached out and touched her cheek and she trembled in my hands.

Once more she didn't respond. Her green eyes were frozen on mind. The silence was unbearable as I didn't know what she thought.

"Hannah..."

"No..." she finally replied.

"What?"

"No, I can't do this. I'm sorry. I like you Deshawn I really do. I love having sex with you, but a relationship? I can't."

"Why not?"

Hannah shook her head, "I don't have to explain why to you. It's my decision. Please just respect it. I have to get back to work." She began to walk away but I got in her way.

"Deshawn move."

"No, tell me why. I deserve more."

"No, I don't have to tell you shit. Now move." She placed her hands on me, attempting to push me back but I didn't budge. "Deshawn move, or I'll kick your ass."

"No, tell me. Tell me why!"

In the limited light of the storage room, I saw the gleam in her eyes, and her bottom lip quivered.

"I can't do this. Not right now. Please Deshawn..."

"Tell me...."

Tears rolled down her cheeks and she shook her head. "Fine. I'll tell you. Asshole..." she wiped her tears away and crossed her arms. "If you really want to know, it's because I'm afraid."

"Afraid of what?"

"I like you Deshawn, I really do, but what if our relationship fizzles out, like the rest of your relationships do? Since having Thomas, I've been careful with the men I bring around the house. Thomas sees you as a friend, and if we get more serious, he might see you as more. If he gets attached, and things with us goes south…"

She paused and wiped her tears away once more.

"I don't want to put him in that pain. He already lives in a broken home, I don't want to have him to experience that. So, the answer is no. I'm sorry. Now move."

"Hannah wait…"

"I said move!" She shoved me hard and I stumbled back.

She growled and stomped past me towards the door.

"Hannah…" I called out to her once more, and she froze. "Hannah I…"

She cut me off and snapped, "I think it's best we don't see each other for a while. You can go. Don't worry about your tab. I'll pay it."

"Hannah…"

"I SAID GO!" She screamed, yanking the door open, pointing out.

I sighed, and looked down, wondering how our relationship became sour so quickly.

Chapter 14

"Ma!" I grinned, opening up my arms, greeting her.

"Deshawn, baby! Its so good to see you!" She grinned, giving me a big hug. She rubbed my back as I stood on the porch of her small home in Norfolk.

"Come in, come in..." she waved me inside her home, and the smell brought me back to the time I was in high school.

After living in low rent housing most my life, my mother saved up enough money to finally put a down payment on a house in the city when I was in high school. The house wasn't much, but it was her home that she owned, and she was proud of it.

Walking it in, it looked like it didn't change a bit as there were multiple pictures of me and her on the wall. She had a new sofa and tv, but for the most part, the living room was set up the same way i remembered.

"Are you hungry?" She asked. "I can fix you a snack or something."

"Nah, I'm good. Besides, I'm taking you out to dinner downtown, remember?"

"Baby, save your money. I can cook something here."

"Ma, it's not that much. I got you."

"Okay," she grinned.

I sat on the sofa, and she sat next to me.

"How's work?" She asked.

"Good, good, good. I got a new client for my firm..." I smirked thinking of Tony, "and they are pretty happy with me."

"That's good."

"What about you? How's your crafting business going?"

She shrugged. "It's going. Busy as ever. I'm glad I quit my job. Between the online orders, and selling at the market, I'm making more than I did working that retail job."

"That's good. I'm glad you're doing what you love."

"Yeah, it's good. Enjoy the free time it brings. Allows me to experience life. Those retail hours were horrible, but owning my own business, I can work when I want."

"That's good."

"So what else is new with you? How things going with that Hannah girl?"

I frowned. "Oh, not so good."

"What happened? You were so confident about her before."

"Well, I told her how I felt, and she didn't feel the same. She was worried about how it would effect her son."

"I told you. When you're a single mother, it's a packaged deal."

"I know ma. I know that. I was ready for that. I really liked her son, and I wasn't afraid to date a woman with a kid."

"Yes, but that's such a big commitment. You're only twenty five."

"So? You always said, I acted older than my age. Between coming home, and cooking myself it taking care of myself when you were working late, I grew up quick. I'm one of the youngest managers at my firm. I may be young, but I'm ready for this commitment."

"True..." my mother paused and patted my knee. "You're really smitten by this woman aren't you?"

"Ma, she's haunts my every thought. Even when we're not together I think of her. I've been a lot of relationships, but this one is different. We're different. I can see a future with her."

"Does she know this?"

"I tried telling her, but as soon as I told her I wanted to be more than friends, she shut down. She didn't want me around and kicked me out."

"Oh...and what did you do afterwards?"

"I gave her space."

"You didn't fight for her?"

"No, she wanted me gone so I left."

She nodded, "let me tell you something. As a single mother, I know how hard it is to date. You're trying to put up these protective walls around your child, hoping that he doesn't see the horrors of the outside world. You care more about your child than yourself and sometimes that's a bad thing. You need to show her how you feel."

"I did ma, she pushed me away."

"So? When someone blocks your shot in basketball, do you give up or do you keep shooting?"

"I keep shooting."

"Exactly. Hannah blocked you, but I know my son. I know you won't just back down when the going gets tough. There's still time left in the game, son. Shoot your shot. Keep shooting until the clock strikes zero. Trust me, she's having her doubts, her main concern is if this relationship is serious or not. Prove to her that you're serious."

I smirked and nodded, feeling more confident. "Okay, I will."

"Good. That's the man I raised." She smiled and stroked my chin.

"Now, let me go get dressed for dinner. We can go in an hour, okay,"

"Yeah, I'd like that. I'll probably head back to DC after dinner. I'm going to go see Hannah when I get back."

"Good. Go get your woman."

I smiled, "thanks ma, I love you."

"I love you too, baby."

She began to walk down the hall, when I called out to her again.

"Hey, ma, was there any man who fought to be in your life when I was a kid?"

"Baby, you and I both know that mama, had two or three men at a time. They couldn't tie me down if they tired."

I snickered and held my gut from laughing hard. "You are too much ma. You are too much."

"You know it," she winked, walking back into her bedroom.

While my mom got dressed to go to dinner, I looked across the room, narrowing my brow. I knew what I had to do. I knew I had to fight for her, and I didn't plan on stopping until she was in my arms.

Chapter 15

When I got back to NoVa area it was a bit past ten. A part of me wanted to go back home, and let Hannah rest, but the other part of me wanted to see her. I knew she was up, as she was a night owl like me.

Parking in her driveway, something felt off as I got out of my car. Her SUV was there, but her front door was slightly open. It was strange because in her neighborhood, you normally don't leave doors open for long.

Walking up to the door, I couldn't shake this feeling of dread. It was like the universe was telling me something was wrong. My senses felt awakened, and the hair on my neck stood as I approached the door.

"Hannah?" I called out.

There was no answer and my heart raced.

"Hannah…" I called at the door. Looking down, I noticed a trail of fresh blood and fear gripped my chest.

"HANNAH!" I screamed, busting into the door. I didn't wait for her to answer. Something was wrong.

Running into her townhome, I found Hannah on the ground. She was covered in blood, her face was cut and busted up.

"Hannah! Dear God…" I muttered, grabbing a hand towel from the kitchen, I rushed to her side, and began wiping the blood off her face.

"Deshawn…what are you doing here?" She asked, teary eyed.

"I wanted to ask for a second chance…but…"

She laughed weakly, "you are too much. You know that."

"I know. What can I say, I just can't take a hint right?" My voice quivered. I didn't know what was wrong with me as I swelled with emotion. "What happened?"

"My ex, Kevin. He came by looking for child support. I was late again. I told, him would get him the money tomorrow. I would get an advance from my boss to pay him, but apparently that wasn't good enough. He tried to take Thomas, even though it was my day. I got in his way." She sighed and closed her eyes as if she was reliving the pain.

I breathed deeply as rage began to flow through my body. I knew what happened next. I could see it on her face and body.

"I got in his way..." she sobbed, wiping her eyes. "I got in his way...he..he...hit me. He didn't stop hitting me. Thomas, cried, trying to push him off me. But Kevin pushed him away. He pushed my son..." she cried out. She banged the floor and shivered breathing deeply. "I couldn't stop him. He was too strong. He just keep hitting me."

All I saw was red. It felt like an out of body experience. Normally I could calm myself down, but in this situation, I couldn't. Rage flowed through me and my eyes narrowed.

"Where is he?" I growled.

"Where is who?"

"Thomas. Where is he?" I repeated.

"He's with Kevin. He lives in Springfield."

"Get in the car. We're going."

"Wait. Deshawn..."

I was already halfway out the door when Hannah followed me, screaming my name.

"Deshawn. Wait. Wait..." she repeated.

I didn't listen. I lost all since of reason. He touched her. He touched her! How dare he touch her...

"Deshawn..." she called out when I stopped at my car.

"Get in..." I repeated.

Hannah didn't argue with me as she ran to the passenger side. She sat in the car and buckled herself in.

"Deshawn. Look at me. What are you going to do?"

I glared at her. "I'm going to get your son back..."

"What are you going to do to Kevin?"

"That choice is his…" I snapped, putting the car into reverse. My tires squealed as in zoomed towards the highway.

Using Hannah's directions I arrived at Kevin's house, and Hannah and I hoped out. In the distance, I could hear Thomas crying and Hannah and I shared a look of concern before she ran up to the house.

"Thomas!" She screamed, running toward the door. She banged on Kevin's door.

"Kevin! Kevin! Let me in. Let in! Don't you dare touch my son. Kevin!"

The door opened, and Kevin glared at Hannah and then looked at me.

"What?"

"I'm coming to get my son."

"Not without paying me first."

"No, he's my son. You're hurting him."

"He's my son. The court said so. He needs to man up."

"Mama…" Thomas cried weakly, walking towards us.

"Thomas!" Hannah cried, shoving Kevin away to pick up her son.

"Let him go! You ain't taking him unless you pay me!"

I growled and shoved Kevin against the wall. "Shut up." I glared. I then looked at Hannah and nodded outside. "Let's go, Hannah. Let's get out here."

Hannah nodded, and clutched her son tightly as as ran out the door towards my car. I held Kevin up to the door as she walked past me.

Kevin laughed. "Look at you. The hero. What you think because you're fucking her, makes you a man now?"

"No what makes me a man, is me not putting my hands on women and children. If ever touch her or her son again, I'll kill you."

"Empty threat. You ain't killing me."

"Test me. For the love of God, please fucking test me." I pushed him hard against the door frame and walked way.

"Hannah, let's go. Get Thomas in the car and..."

"Deshawn, watch out!" Hannah cried out.

I turned around only to see Kevin punching me in the face. I reared around, clutching my chin from his sucker punch. That was the only hit I allowed. From there I saw red.

I tackled him to the ground, and started pummeling him. Rage coursed through me, as my fists connected to his face. I wasn't in control. I couldn't stop myself. All I wanted was blood, and I was having it, as I caved his face in.

In the distance I heard Hannah yelled and telling me to get off, but I didn't. No I kept going. The fucker needed to learn. He needed to understand that I wasn't messing around when I told him he couldn't touch her again. That image of her bruised and beaten replayed in my mind. I wasn't there for her. He was going to pay for hurting her. He was going to *fucking pay*.

I heard the sirens and saw the lights. I felt strong hands on me as multiple people pulled me away. I was laying face down in the grass, as a cops knee was on my back.

"Settle down. Settle down! Let me see your hands. Give me your hands!" The cop yelled at me. I felt the cold steel wrap around my wrist, and was picked up, only to see Kevin coughing blood and being placed on the stretcher.

"Don't you ever touch her again. You hear me! Don't you ever touch HER!" I yelled, being dragged away.

The fucker was lucky the cops came. I would've finished the job. As I was taken towards the cop car, I looked at Hannah who still clutched Thomas close to her chest. Tears rolled down her eyes looking at me. I smiled at her before being shoved into the car.

I didn't know what my punishment was for nearly killing Kevin, but I'd gladly pay it. For her it was worth the cost. For her, I would go to hell and back.

Chapter 16

Sitting in the the jail cell, I stare at my busted up knuckles. adrenaline still pumped through me as I took long winded breaths. I could still feel the phantom pain of my fists hitting Kevin's face.

The last hour had been a whirlwind, between being booked for for the crime of aggravated assault, and being fingerprint and photographed, it was a journey I never thought I'd made. My ma made sure I kept my nose clean, and off the street. She didn't want me to end up in jail, yet here I was, in a dark twisted way, I was fulfilling my destiny as a black man in this country.

However, this was my choice to be here. I knew that being charged with aggravated assault was a felony and I could be looking at a year of jail time, but I didn't care. Hannah was safe. That fucker was in the hospital. I taught him a lesson he would never forget.

Touch her and die.

The rules were simple. No man nor God could stop my wrath if he comes near her again.

Sitting in the cell, I didn't know what came next for me. I knew I had my bail hearing in a few hours, and from there, I'd probably learn my fate. Knowing that the bail would be ridiculous, I figured I'd probably would have to at least get a loan to get out of jail. Speaking of loans, I have no idea how my job is going to react to me being locked up. I'm sure they won't be happy that one of their financial managers is a felon. I'm sure that's great for business. All the clients would be lining up for the felon on the staff. Perhaps they could start a new criminal division where I only work with other clients who've been charge with white collar crime or want to deal with under the table shady businesses.

I chuckled thinking of the business idea when the sheriff deputy tapped in the bar across from me.

"What's so funny?" He asked.

"Nothing. Just thinking about my life when I get out."

He nodded and then placed the key in the gate, "well then todays your lucky day. Bails been paid. You're free to go."

"Already? I didn't even get a hearing."

"Appears, you got some friends in high places. Come on, I don't got all night."

I stood, and allowed the sheriff to uncuff me. Walking down the hall, I tried to figure out who I knew had that type of pull on town, but the moment I saw his greased up slick black hair, I knew who pulled the strings.

Tony saw me and grinned, walking towards me. "Deshawn! You're okay?" He asked, patting my back. He was in black fabric sweatsuit, with a white tank top underneath. As usual it looked like he was wearing every piece of jewelry he owned.

"Yeah, I'm good. Did you bail me out?"

"Yeah, the moment you got taken away, Hannah called me. "

"Hannah, is she okay?"

"Yeah, she's fine. Just shaken up. That's all. Vicki took her to the hospital and is watching Thomas while she gets stitched up. Come on let's outta here. I'll drive you home."

"Thanks." He nodded his and I followed him down the hall towards the exit.

"That's good that she's okay. I was worried about her." I replied.

"She was worried about you too."

I couldn't help but smile.

We walked out the door, towards, Tony's sports car parked in the front. I got into the passenger side while Tony sat on the driver's side. He started up the car and drove away from the courthouse. Once we got on the highway, Tony looked at me and said, "Hannah is pressing charges too."

I opened my eyes wide staring at Tony.

"Yeah, she's had enough of her ex. With her testimony, and her kid's, they have enough to get the judge to grant her full custody of Thomas."

"That's good."

"Yeah, it is."

"Thanks for paying my bail by the way. I'll pay you back."

Tony waved me off. "Nah, you're good. We didn't know about Hannah and her relationship problems. In our group we normally don't talk to much about our normal lives, we should've saw the signs of abuse. What you did for her..." he shook his head. "You have to understand, Vicki and I love Hannah. You saving her and her son, that's a debt that we can't repay. You're a good man, Deshawn. Don't let anyone tell you otherwise."

"Thanks, I'm not looking forward to hearing about this from my job on Monday though. I'm sorry, but I'm afraid I'm probably not going to be managing your account there anymore with my potential felony charge."

"Felony?"

"Yeah, they told me I was being booked with aggravated assault."

"Nah, talked to the judge. He's a good friend of mine. Likes to fuck my wife every now and again..." Tony said nonchalantly, with a shrug. "As soon as I explained the situation to him, he dropped the charge to a simple assault. At most you're looking at some community service or a fine."

"Wow, you serious?"

"Yeah, that's what friends are for."

"Thanks, Tony."

Tony winked at me, and placed his blinker in to exit the highway near my apartment . "Also don't worry about your job."

"Yeah, but your account has a couple of million in it. I won't be managing it. You signed a contract to keep your money there for at least a year. And I can't work with you for at least three years…"

"Like I said. Don't worry. It's only a couple of mil. Shit I make that in a month. You'll come work for me at my firm."

"Wait are you serious?"

"Yeah, you're smart, a go getter, not afraid to take any shit. You'd be a great lobbyist. We are always looking for you finance types. Work for me, and I'll double what ever you were making at firm."

"Wow…Tony…"

"Is that a yes?"

"Of course. I can't thank you enough."

Tony parked at my apartment and smiled, "no you already have. You saved Hannah and that little boy. You deserve a heroes bounty, and that's what I'm going to give you. I'll see you soon. I'll have my assistant email you details on the job, okay?"

"Yeah, definitely. Thanks." I unbuckled my seat belt and began to get out of the car when Tony called out for me.

"Oh and hey, Deshawn. My wife and I are having another get together next week. She wants you to come by. I don't know what you did to her, but she's still talking about that dick of yours."

I laughed. "Yeah, I'm there."

"Good. See you around, kid."

I shut the door to his sports car and watched him speed way. I couldn't stop smiling. Just when I thought my life was over, I got thrown a second chance and I didn't plan on wasting it.

Chapter 17

Walking back to my apartment , I didn't expect to see her. Hannah was leaning against the wall, waiting for me by my door. She was wearing a pair of yoga pants and a tank top, with her hair in a messy bun. Her face was cleaned up, stitched up and bandaged. She still had bruises on her cheek and eyes from Kevin's assault, but to me, she never looked more beautiful.

"Hi..." she whispered, walking towards me.

"Are you okay?" We both asked at the same time.

She looked down at her feet and blushed. "Sorry, you go first."

"No, you go first. It's cool..."

She bit her lip and then nodded towards my door, "can we go inside and talk?"

"Yeah, sure."

I unlocked my apartment door and then let Hannah inside. She looked around my place, and then stared back at me.

"Where's Thomas?" I asked.

"Vicki said she'd watch him for the night."

"Ah, that was nice of her."

"Yeah, he's a bit shaken up after everything."

I would imagine. "How are you?"

"Still processing everything. After you were arrested, I called the police and had Kevin place under arrest for domestic violence and child endangerment. Tony is getting me a lawyer who says, I'll be able to win full custody of Thomas."

"That's good. Yeah, Tony is looking out for me too. He got my charges dropped to a misdemeanor and offered me a job at his firm too."

"That's good."

"Yeah, I'm glad we have Tony in our lives. He really saved us."

"No, you saved us. You stuck up for me, when no one else would. You protected me and Thomas. You fought for us. You nearly went to jail for us.

"And I'll do it all in a heartbeat again if I was given a chance."

I took a step towards her, and Hannah shivered the closer I got.

"Are you okay? Are you cold?"

"No, I'm fine. I'm good. Just a stray shiver..."

I reached up and rubbed her arm. "Better?"

"Yeah better..." She inched closer to me, placing her hands around my waist, and her head on my chest. The smell of her perfume felt like reuniting with an old friend. It had only been a few hours since I last held her, but it felt like an entirety in the time.

Holding her, I whispered, "I love you..."

She leaned her head back and her eyes opened wide. Her jaw dropped and her green eyes shined in the limited light of my apartment.

"Deshawn, I..."

"You don't have to say it back. Hell, you don't have to do a thing. I just wanted you to know. I don't care about our relationship status. I don't give a damn if we're friends, fuck buddies or girlfriend and boyfriend. I just don't care. All I know is I want you in my life. I want Thomas in my life. If you don't want that, that's fine, but know I'm not going to give up on you. I'm going to keep fighting for you. I am going to keep fighting until..."

My words were halted when Hannah pressed her lips upon mine. I was shocked at first as I stood frozen in place, but I soon placed my hands around her, deepening our kiss.

She breathed deeply, placing her head on mine. "I love you too..." she admitted.

"Hannah..."

"I do. I really do. I was afraid before. I was afraid of the unknown of us being together. I didn't want to lose you out of my life if things went bad, but now I know you're going to fight of us. You're going to fight for me. I was afraid to admit this before, but now I know. I know with all of my heart, I love you..."

"Hannah..."

My lips crashed into hers yet again. She moaned as my tongue slipped into her mouth, and twisted with hers. Holding her by her ass, I picked her up, and Hannah wrapped her legs around my torso.

Our passion for each other did the talking. Not a word was share, just emotional touch. She touched me. I touched her. I kissed her neck. She kissed my neck. We were inseparable. We didn't want to break a part for a moment. We spent far to much time a part, and all we wanted to was spend the rest of our time with each other.

"Deshawn..." she muttered.

"Yes..."

"Take me to our bed..." her voice was filled with urgent need as I carried her to my bedroom.

I kicked open my door like a madman and tossed her into the mattress. She grabbed the hem of her top and tossed it off, while I removed my shirt and jeans. I helped her with her yoga pants, revealing her soaking mound. My cock stiffened from the sight.

Leaning forward, I nuzzled my head into her folds, licking and sucking her cunt. She moaned, placing her hand on my head, allowing me to bury my head deeper into her region.

"Deshawn, I want you. Please make love to me."

"Okay, let me grab a condom."

"No..." she grabbed my hand and shook her head. "No condom. I want to feel you. I want to feel all of you."

"Are you sure?" I asked.

"Whatever happens, happens, but right now, I know I want to make love to the man who loves me."

"Fuck Hannah..." I leaned forward and kissed her. Breaking a part, I breathed, "I fucking love you so much."

"I know."

Grabbing my dick, I aimed her center and slipped it in. Fuck me did she feel good. That warm wetness covered my cock. I was in heaven as she swallowed me whole. I was engulfed in pleasure and I didn't want to leave.

Laying on top of her, I sensually pumped in and out of her. There were no extra moves. No doggy style, nor cowgirl or side fucks. It was straight missionary, but it was not an ordinary missionary . This missionary was loving and tender. This missionary was passionate and breath taking.

There was a fire between us. One that was lit by power of love. She wanted me. I wanted her. It wasn't just about the sex. No we moved past that. It was more about the sex. It was about connection. It was about love. What we shared in that bed was magical.

We were consumed with each other, kissing and touching each other in various places. I squeezed her breasts, she squeezed my ass. I kissed her neck. She kissed my lips. Our gasps filled the air as the bed softly creaked from me rocking.

"Deshawn...oh...god..." she whispered.

She closed her eyes and shivered. Her whole body seemed possessed as it trembled. She breathed deeply and her eyes locked on mine. Goddamn was it a sexy look.

I growled and devoured her lips once more. Holding her hips, I buried every inch I had into her. Fuck was she slick. I slipped in and out of her with ease, and I loved the feeling of skin on skin contact.

My senses were on overload. My mind was on fire, and my body was ready to explode. I was nearly there.

"I am about to pop. I going to pull out..."

"No wait...stay." She held me tighter.

"Are you sure?"

She nodded.

"Okay...I'll stay..." I kissed her once more and seconds later, I came, filling her up with my seed. I continued to pump into her until I was limp. When I was through, I pulled out of her watching as my cum leaked out of her pussy onto the mattress.

"Hey, come here..." she waved me close and I laid back down next to her. Breathing deeply.

"That was wonderful." I gasped.

"It was."

"I'm so happy that you're mine."

"I love you, Deshawn."

"I love you with all my heart, Hannah."

Chapter 18

Three months later

Carrying a box, I looked around the empty three story townhome. It was strange being a home owner. I never saw myself as one, until now.

Now I have a family to look after. Granted, Hannah and I weren't married, but we might as well be as she agreed to move in with me.

I'm glad her and Thomas no longer live in the slums. I was worried about them being on their own, and now, under one roof, we can all be together.

I walked past the large living space, into the open concept kitchen and placed the box marked kitchen onto the white marble countertop.

I really loved how the townhouse had ample light and the pale oak hardwood floors, plus there was three bedrooms, an office and a double shower bathroom master bathroom, for those nights where Hannah and I wanted to get a little frisky and shower at the same time, Our new home was located in a new posh neighborhood in McLean, and it was a perfect place to raise a kid, as there was a playground nearby, along with some of the the best schools in the district. Everything was perfect.

Hannah walked behind me carrying, another box and placing it beside me.

Sweat covered her brow as it was a warm summer day, and she wore her hair in a tight ponytail pushed back by a headband. Like me, she wore shorts, except hers were shorter than mine, ending at the mid thigh, showing her sexy tattooed thick legs, and unlike me, she had on a tank top, with a sports bra underneath, while I just had on an old Washington shirt. Damn did she look sexy in her outfit. I know I say this often, but you just had to be there. Sweat glistening off her skin, eyes shadowed eyes, smooth lip glossed lips, and her ass nearly hanging out her short shorts. Fuck me, I've had a mid cub since I first laid eyes on her his morning.

"Is that all you carried?" She asked walking into the kitchen. "Aren't you supposed to be the man in this relationship? I feel like my box was heavier than yours..." she touched my box trying to compare the two.

"Hey, I'm just getting started. It's about pace. I wouldn't want to blow my load too early."

"Trust me, I have ways to make you blow your load..." she kissed me and fondled my cock.

"Damn, girl. If we start fooling around, we ain't never going to get this place done."

"I know. I know. Come on, let's get the rest of this stuff in."

I nodded and followed her back out to the moving van. My mom had came up from Norfolk, and she had helped us by taking Thomas up to the national monuments, giving Hannah and I time to move our stuff into the the new house.

Taking a step up to the storage truck, I helped Hannah up, and she looks around at the jammed back moving van.

"What did you want to carry next?"

"Well, we got all the kitchen stuff. Did you want to work on the dining room next?"

"Yeah, we can do that."

"Okay, help me with this table..." I dragged the table out and flipped it upright for Hannah to grab the other end. She grunted and held her end, while I held mine. Walking backwards, I led her into the doorway, and paused for a moment.

"Tilted it to the left."

"This way?"

"Yeah, like that." I walked back and accidentally scrapped the walk. "Shit, go back, go back."

"What happened?"

"We bumped into the wall and made a mark."

She laughed. "Aww, aren't we making this place homey. Our first scuff dent."

"We should get it framed."

I laughed. "Okay, let's try it again."

We adjusted the table and were able to get it fully inside this time.

"Great, let's put it over here, in front of the breakfast bar."

"Yep..."

We placed the table down and Hannah gasped. "It looks nice."

"Yeah, it does. It's a little out of place though. It doesn't really match the color scheme."

"Look at you. All Home TV."

"I'm just saying it would be nice to have matching furniture. Instead of the mismatch stuff we have."

"Deshawn, I don't want you to overextend yourself with all of this. I mean, your paying for this townhouse already. I don't want you to go into financial trouble trying to live this lavish lifestyle."

"I can afford it."

"Are you sure? I already feel bad that I can't help out with the mortgage."

"It's fine. Really it is."

"But moving in. It's such a big step..."

"Hannah we've been through this. I didn't want you living in that neighborhood anymore. It wasn't safe. It's safe here. Okay?"

"Yeah, I know. It's so quiet though. Where's the sirens, the random hip hop song being blasted by a car or home, or the bums walking around. I miss my trash blowing down the street." She muttered, placing her head on my chest.

I chuckled, "you've been upgraded to home associations and preppy moms in yoga pants speed walking."

"God, give me the bums over the rich housewives. If I ever turn into one of them, shoot me."

"Never, housewives are sexy."

"God, you would. I swear everything turns you on."

"I'm a guy. If it has a hole, I'm fucking it."

She rolled her eyes laughing. "God you are too much. I love you."

"I love you too." I gave her a quick peck kiss, and held her by her ass. She placed her head in my chest and wrapped her hands round my back.

"Are you sure this house isn't too much?"

"Yes! Hannah why do you keep asking?"

"Because, I'm worried. We aren't married. We haven't made any vows or anything. I just don't want to see you alone in this place."

"Alone? You'd be with me."

"But if things don't work out between us."

"Why would you even put that in the air?"

"I'm sorry, I know things have been good between us, but you said it yourself, your relationships don't last. If ours fizzes out..."

I grab her face cheeks and kiss her. "This relationship won't fizzle out. I love you."

"I love you too, but I'm just scared. What if this one ends like the others."

"This one won't. This one is different."

"I just have this stray feeling I can't get away from..."

I shushed her, placing a finger on her lips. "Enough. Enough. Today is a big step for us. Let's focus on that. Besides, we haven't properly christened this place. My mom has Thomas for the next two hours, and I intend to fuck you in every room in this house. Starting with the kitchen..." I leaned forward and sucked on her neck.

"Deshawn... we don't have time for this..."

"There's always time for a quickie..." I licked her skin and palmed her breasts, massaging it in my hand.

"Deshawn...Fuck...you are too bad for me..."

"I know, don't lie you like it…" my hand slipped past the waistband into her shorts. Her folds were wet and dripping. She fell onto my finger, moaning.

"Deshawn…Fuck Deshawn…" she grabbed my chin and kissed me back, my hand continued to fondle her, slipping in and out of the greased hole. I pushed her back towards the kitchen counter, and we our bodies collided with the marble, I pulled her shorts down to her ankles and fell to my knees to suck her succulent outer lips. Fuck me did she taste good. There's nothing like slurping on her juices.

She pushed my head deep into her crevice. Her foot stomped on the ground, as my tongue slithered in and out of her. I made sure not a drop of her juice touched the floor. It was too damn good to waste.

"Right there…right there…fuckk…." She squealed, her body twisted in my hands, but I kept her in one place, continuing the assault on her sweet spot.

I pulled away and there was a small whimper in her lips.

"Don't give me that look." I smirked.

"You didn't finish me."

"You need to share. Get that ass up on that counter."

She smiled and I helped her towards the edge of the top.

"Oh, I like how the marble feels on my ass."

"Good choice on the marble?"

"Yeah, great choice," she grinned kissing me. As our lips stayed connected, she pushed my shorts down and clutched my hard cock. She gave it a few tugs before slipping into her juicy slit. I groaned and pumped in and out of her. Moaning, she wrapped her arms around me, taking every inch I thrusted into her. Our sex noises echoed in the kitchen as we took each other.

"Damn, I'm slipping…" she laughed.

"What's wrong?"

"My ass is covered the marble in sweat. I keep slipping."

"Here…" I picked her off the counter and carried her to the stairs. Sitting down, I held her waist and slapped her ass.

"Your turn. Ride it."

"With pleasure." She bounced on my cock, and I held her waist looking up at her. I loved watching her tits jiggle. Even in the tank top and sports bra, her big breasts still managed to shake.

She took me fast and hard on the stairwell. As she rode me, she grabbed the banister, screaming. Her words were inaudible as if she was speaking in tongues.

I slapped her ass and growled, "yeah that's it. Take that dick. Take it. It's fucking yours."

My words were like lighter fluid for her as her pace quickened.

"Goddamn." I slapped her ass and then picked her up once more, placing her down on the hardwood floor. Getting on my side, Hannah did the same, laying on her left side. She left a leg up allowing me to get into position. Our bodies molded together on the floor. Both of us moaning as each other's pleasures grew.

Looking into Hannah's eyes I smiled as I came inside her. When I was through, I pulled out of her watching as my cum leaked out of her into the hardwood floor.

"It's so nice of you to share your creampie, with the house."

"Haha. Give me a towel. I need to wipe this out."

"Towels are still in the truck."

"And this is why I wanted to get everything out first before we fucked."

"Admit it, it was hot."

"Yeah, it was steamy. I'm happy we did it. It's just now I'm sticky and we didn't even move a thing."

I leaned forward and kissed her. "How about this, we shower, get this funk of lust off us, and then continue moving."

"I'd like that."

"Good, because it's a duel shower, and I've been waiting to take a shower with you all day."

"Then what are we waiting for. Let's go." She took off her tank top and bra and tossed it at me, becoming completely naked. I grinned and removed my own clothes chasing her down naked in our brand new house together.

I knew what she said about my prior relationships were true, they did fizzle out, but I also knew this relationship I had with her was special, and I wasn't planning on giving up on that.

Chapter 19

Rubbing my eyes, I sighed, starting at the computer screen. I really hated working on this project.

Yes, the money was great, but at what cost? At my old firm, I didn't put in as many hours as I did at Tony's lobbyist firm. It seemed like I was working 28 hours a day with no breaks.

Even worse, I felt like I was losing Hannah. All of my free time was spent working. I worked seven days a week, with very little down time. I missed hanging out with her and Thomas. Before, we would go on walks in the neighborhood. We would play toys and chase each other around the house. Now I'm stuck either in my office or my home office working.

Part of me wanted to quit. I wanted to tell Tony to fuck off and be with Hannah and Thomas, while the other knew I had to have this job. Without this job, I could afford the mortgage. I knew Hannah couldn't support us with her tips she made at the bar. I was stuck between a rock and a hard place with nowhere to go.

Sighing, I continued to work, crunching numbers on my ten key when Hannah came down the stairs into the living room. I didn't look at her, as my eyes stayed trained on my computer screen in front of me.

"Hey babe, I put Thomas to sleep."

"That's good. He was a bit cranky..." I replied.

"He was just tired. As soon as I got his milk and read him a story, he was passed out."

She walked up behind me and rubbed my shoulders. I smiled smelling her sweet perfume. I sighed and placed my hand on hers and then kissed her palm.

"You're still working? I thought you'd be done by now."

"Same, but a partner just emailed me. Asked me to look into some things."

Hannah sighed, "is Tony that strict?"

"Nah, Tony works in a different division. I'm working for a different partner."

"Have you thought about transferring to Tony's division? I doubt Tony would be this brutal."

"I have, but I'm the new guy around the office. I didn't want to make it seem like I was Tony's pet earning favors. I wanted to earn my respect my own way."

"I gotcha. When do you think you'd be done?"

"Honestly, I don't know. I think it's going to be another late one."

"That's the third late night in a row. You promised tonight would be our night."

"I know babe. I know did, but this job. Has me…I have to keep working. Tomorrow, okay? I promise tomorrow."

"Fine…"

She kissed my cheek and I heard her walk away. Once she was gone I continued to work. In the background, I heard her walk up the stairs, the shower turn on, and shuffling in our bedroom. I wondered what she was doing, but my mind didn't drift for long as I refocused on my work.

I was engulfed in the project, when I heard Hannah come back downstairs. Once again, I didn't look at her as I typed away.

I heard the tv turn on and the dvd tray opening. I guess she was going to watch a movie. That was fine, it would be nice to have some background noise while I worked.

I heard a familiar upbeat techno song, and I tilted my head as the music sounded familiar. I heard moans coming from the tv and I turned to see what she was watching. To my surprise, a mature woman was getting railed by a big dicked black dude on screen.

Hannah was sprawled out on the couch wearing sexy lingerie, including a lace bra, garter belt, and stockings. She didn't bother wearing any panties as her shaved mound was displayed for me to see. Sitting beside her was a large black dildo, lube and a bullet vibrator. She quietly fingered herself as she used the controller to pick a porn scene.

"Hannah...what are you doing..." I breathed. My eyes didn't leave her silky white skin.

"Well, you were busy and I was horny. Decided to take care of business myself." She turned back to the tv and selected a scene. "Oh, I like this porn star. His dick is so fucking big." After choosing the scene, the movie started, with a black plumper ringing a doorbell. A busty bbw dressed in a sexy mini dress walked up to the door to answer it. While the movie was playing, Hannah grabbed her small bullet vibrator and started to play herself.

My cock tented in my sweats, watching Hannah rub her body.

"Baby, you don't have worry, I got this. Go back to work."

I breathed heavily. All I wanted to do was have her. I knew my work needed to be done, at the same time her curvy body was like a siren calling out to me.

She moaned and titled her head back, watching as the white bbw got in her knees and started sucking the black man. I had to admit it was hot watching my girlfriend masturbate to porn. It was overwhelming to my visual senses as I was caught between wanting to watch the porn on screen and wanting to watch her pleasure herself.

I simply stood there, watching as she got off.

"Baby..it's fine. Go work." She grunted.

I didn't want to work. Not tonight. Not with her like this.

"Babe, work can wait. Let's fuck..."

"No, you said you had an important project. Go over there and work. Don't you dare come over here and touch me."

My jaw dropped as all I wanted to do was be buried into her folds.

"Babe..."

"Don't babe me. It's obviously important that you get your job done. Go. Work." She shooed me away, and I groaned.

I didn't want to work. Not right now. Not seeing her like this. Her body on display was a tease to my eyes. My cock burned as it was harder than stone. I had to relieve myself.

The porn movie continued, and the black man had the woman laying in her back. Her legs were opened wide as he feverishly devoured her pussy, eating her out like a madman.

Hannah moaned and rubbed her tit. Her hand continued to jiggle down below, plunging deeper into her folds.

"Fuck me..." I groaned. My cock yearned to be touched. It twitched and leaked precum as it my stiffness bent my will. I knew what needed to be done, but she had me under her spell. A desire burned deep within me. I couldn't stop myself.

My hand crept into my sweats and I stroked myself watching her. I breathed deeply, simulated by the sound of the porn, and sexy images of Hannah fucking herself with the black dildo and the plump bbw getting railed from behind on screen.

I groaned, rubbing my full length to the erotic scene in front of me. Damn did Hannah look sexy in her lingerie. I loved how her fabric fit her curves. It highlighted every inch of her smooth white skin. Her bra pushed up her tits, making them look twice as large, and my eyes couldn't stray from watching her painted toenails point to the ceiling as she slipped the dildo deeper in her pussy.

My mouth watered, waiting to taste her supple skin. My cock twitched wanting to be buried in her wetness. My fingers burned wanting to squeeze and knead her breasts. She was a delicacy to my senses, and a need that I wanted but couldn't have.

"Fuck..." I growled. Lust consumed me. I wanted her. I wanted her badly.

She looked up and grinned as if this was her plan along.

"I though you had to work."

"Fuck work... I want you."

"I'm still not letting you fuck me."

"Why not?"

"Because your being punished. You ignored me. So I'm ignoring you."

"Baby please. Please let me fuck you."

"No, you can watch, but you can't touch."

I growled. I hated the idea of watching her. I wanted to join her. I wanted to feel her. I wanted to fuck her.

My hand quickly jerked my hard length. I bit my lip as I was coming near my limit.

"Don't you dare come either."

"What?" I gasped.

"Don't come."

"Or else what?"

"Or else you won't get your surprise…"

"Which is what?"

"My ass…" she adjusted herself on the couch and revealed the butt plug she was wearing.

"I put in in upstairs."

"Fuck…" I whispered, looking at the silicone plug inside her pink puckered hole.

She sat back up and leaned on the sofa to looked me in the eye. "You're in timeout for the next three minutes. If you come, while jerking off, then back to work. If you don't then you can come over and play…"

"Fuck me…" I groaned, my pace slowed attempting avoid the inevitable.

"Nope. Keep going. Faster."

"That's unfair…"

"I set the rules."

I bit my lip and breathed, trying to control my body's urges.

"Come closer." She beckoned, waving me close. I walked towards the edge of the sofa where she sat up, giving me a naughty grin. "Did you want to apologize to me?"

"Apologize?"

"Yes, you left me alone. You chose work over me, and now, you're being punished for it. Are you sorry?"

"Yes…" I whimpered.

"Are you sure about that?"

"Yes, I'm sorry…"

"Hmm…how bad do you want to fuck my ass?"

"Badly. I want to be in there so bad right now."

"Are you going to come right now?"

"No…"

"What about now…" she grabbed my cock and placed it in her mouth. She deep throated me and I closed my eyes gasping for air.

"Fuucccckkk…."

She popped my dick out of her mouth and keep jerking me off. "Don't you dare come. Don't you fucking do it."

I was at the edge. I couldn't stop it. It was a painful pleasure keeping my cum at bay. My fingers twitched. My body felt numb. It wanted a release, but I fought with everything I had to keep it back.

"I can't hold it anymore…"

"That's a shame. No ass for you today….I'm going to suck you off again. You better not come in my mouth."

"Fuck…"

She placed me in her mouth once more and sucked on my cock. She fondled my balls, gurgling on my length as she took me halfway.

I breathed deeply. All I wanted to do was come, but I also wanted to feel the tight cavity of her ass too.

She popped my dick out of her mouth and jerked it off.

"Hmm… times up. Your timeout is over. Are you ready to fuck me?"

"Yes…please…"

"Good. Come over here. Lube up your cock..."

I took off my pants and hustled over to the couch. Grabbing the lube, I quickly lathered myself up.

"Sit." She instructed, and I sat on the couch, watching as she pulled the plug from her asshole. I groaned, looking at her gaping hole. Placing her feet on my thighs, she sat on my cock, slipping it inside her ass, and squatted down. Damn did she feel good. Her ass was a vice grip around my cock.

She slowly bounced up and down my hard cock. I groaned watching as my dick slipped inside her plump curvy ass. I smirked as a trail of lube dripped down my hard black shaft onto the floor. She leaned on me, moaning as she rode me anally. Reaching down to her wet core, I fingered her watching as she rode my length.

"Use the dildo..." she breathed.

I reached out for the fake black cock and plunged it inside her pussy. She moaned, being double stuffed the dildo and my cock. I moved with her, thrusting my cock into her ass, while shoving the big toy into her folds.

She moaned, and I felt her warm sweaty body on mine. I smiled, smelling her sweet wet musk and the tickle of her red hair on my nose as she arched her back. I slight bit her neck, tasting her sweaty flesh, making my mark on her. She was mine. She was all fucking mine.

I loved her plump ass. Her thick cheeks gave her an extra bounce not to mention it was a feast for my eyes watching her curves jiggle. I was in heaven as my cock felt like it was being sucked dry by her ass.

"How does it feel to be doubled stuffed?"

"Good. Fuck, I've missed you."

"I missed you too baby."

"I wanted your cock for the last couple of days now."

"I know. I know. I'm here now. I'm here."

"Then take me. Fucking take me. Make me come. Please let me come."

I quickened my pace with her dildo jerking it in and out of her as fast as I could. She gasped and then yelled as she'd body took wave after wave of pleasure.

My balls trembled and seconds later, I came filling her cavity up with my cum. When I was through, I pulled out of her watching as her ass hole leak my white seed.

"Fuck...that was hot." I gasped.

"It was. Wasn't it."

"I love you." I smiled, brushing a stray hair away from her face.

"I love you too." She grinned. She kissed me, "promise me you won't forget about me. We need to make time for each other okay,"

"Yeah; I gotcha. Perhaps after a certain time I stop working."

"That could work." She kissed me and we both laid down on the couch, cuddling.

"This is nice. You holding me like this."

"Yeah, I like it too." Hannah looked into my eyes and smiled. We shared a tender moment until we heard, "stuff me with your black cock daddy!"

Looking back at the tv, another porn scene was on, with a milf being plugged by two black dicks.

We both laughed, and Hannah said "I totally forgot this was on."

"Me too..." I grinned.

"Did you want to watch it?"

"Yeah, I'd love too."

Hannah smiled, and cuddled closer to me, rubbing her ass into my crotch. As we laid there watching porn, I was reminded of what I had with Hannah. She was no ordinary woman, and for that I loved her.

Chapter 20

I should be focusing on her but I'm not.

No my mind is somewhere else. It's fixated on something other than her beautiful smile and her voluptuous curves. Physically, I'm here. I am inches into her, thrusting hard into her, but mentally I'm not there. No, I'm thinking about my job. I'm thinking about my job and how I can write up the project I was working on.

Two weeks ago, I made Hannah a promise to be more transparent, but I feel like I'm breaking that promise. Her and Thomas were supposed to be my number one, but now they feel like a distant second. I tried to put Hannah in the spotlight. I tried to make time for her, but my job kept pulling me away. It kept taking the spot that should've belonged to her.

I should be enjoying this. I mean, look at her. Fuck me was she sexy. Her red hair was matted down on the mattress. Her tits jiggled with every strike from me. Her smooth legs rested in my shoulders as I pumped into her.

This is what I loved about her. Yet, I'm not appreciating it. I couldn't because my mind continued to drift. I continued to think about things that are out of my control. Why am I'm plagued with these thoughts. I should be feeling pleasure, yet all I feel is despair.

I am drowning at my job. I can't catch a break. All I want is to be with Hannah, yet I can't. I can't slip away.

"Right there. Right there..." she moaned. She gasped. "Fuck! That feels good Deshawn. Fuck me. Fuck me harder, baby."

I didn't reply to her. My mind was elsewhere.

"Deshawn, baby...are you okay?" She asked reaching up to touch me.

"Yeah, I'm good. I'm good." I repeated.

"Yeah, but..."

I didn't say anything as I finished early and pulled out of her. She laid on her back quietly studying me, as I laid beside her breathing deeply.

Placing one hand on her head, she propped herself up and looked into my eyes, "Deshawn what aren't you telling me? Is something wrong?"

"No, everything is fine." I mumbled.

"Okay...sex was good. I liked it." She whispered, placing her head on my chest. "It's okay you came early. We can go again soon."

"Actually...I'm done for tonight. I'm going back to work."

"Deshawn it's after ten. You promised after ten is our time. No work."

"I know, but this project. It's a lot more than I thought it was. The partner wants it done, as soon as possible." I rolled out of bed, placing my sweats and a T-shirt on.

Hannah sat up in bed, watching my every move.

"You're always working."

"I'm sorry, baby, it's just...this job is tough and demanding. Trust me if I could stay in bed with you, I could."

"You promised that after ten was our time..." she repeated. "Why do you do this, why won't you make time for me."

I chuckled, shaking my head.

"Why are you laughing," she snapped, narrowing her brow.

"I've made time for you. For the last two weeks, I held my promise. Not to mention, anytime you need something, I'm there. Every time Thomas needs me, I'm there. I'm always there. For one second, would you give me a break? It's hard enough trying to take care of Thomas. He's always needing something."

"That's the gig, Deshawn. That's parenting in a nutshell. We don't get no breaks. Do you think I ever get a break?"

"Yeah, but Thomas isn't my kid..." the moment I said the words I regretted it.

She scoffed. "What's that supposed to mean?" Her voice got louder.

"I'm sorry, it's not what I meant ..."

"No, I think I knew exactly what you meant. Typical, what you think you can only play house when things are going good? Rising a child is more than just playing toys. It's a lot more than that." She snapped.

I opened my mouth to reply, but I heard a voice down the hall from Thomas.

"Mommy..." he called out.

"Great you woke him up." She sighed.

"I got him..." I replied, walking towards the door.

"No, I got him..." she snapped, quickly getting dressed in a tank top and shorts. "He asked for Mommy, not Deshawn. You've been excused from your so called *parenting* duties."

She walked towards the door where I stood and placed her hands on her hips. "Move, I have to go check on him."

I growled frustrated and stepped to the side.

"Oh, and by the way, since you are feeling so inclined to work tonight, just stay downstairs and sleep on the sofa."

"Hannah..." I began to say, but she didn't reply as she stomped down the hall towards Thomas' room.

I shook my head and walk away. "Fuck her..." I growled feeling emotional. She had no idea how much stress I was under. She didn't care to listen. What is going on with our relationship?

Chapter 21

I still felt a bad about our fight. I felt like the worlds biggest asshole. Why did I say those things about Thomas? I loved Thomas just as much as I loved Hannah. If I could go back in time and take back the things I said, I could.

I left the townhouse early in the morning before Hannah and Thomas could wait up. I honestly didn't know what to say to them. How do you make up for being the worlds biggest asshole.

Hannah deserves better than me.

I sighed, and tapped my keyboard working through the report at my office. While I wasn't in a large corner office, I did have an office of my own. Perks of being a top member of the firm.

Office door was closed when I heard knock.

"I'm busy…" I muttered not looking away from my screen.

"It's Hannah…" the voice responded.

"Hannah?" I stood and opened the door for her. Damn did she look breathing taking in her mini dress and heels. The dress was strapless, allowing me to see her busty cleavage, and the dress was cut at the mid thigh, giving a glimpse of her plump ass.

"What are you doing here," I breathed, my eyes still lingering on her curves.

"Do you have a second to talk?"

"Yeah, come in."

She came into my office and I closed the door behind her.

"Take a seat…" I offered, pulling out a chair. She sat down and I sat in the desk next to her. From my high vantage point, I could see a perfect view of her tits, and upper thighs. My cock twitches from erotic view.

"I hope I'm not bothering you."

"No, I have a few minutes."

"Good, I just wanted to talk to you about last night. We never got a chance to settle things, and you left early this morning so we couldn't talk."

"Yeah, I just wanted to say I'm sorry. About the things I said about Thomas... I don't mean it. I love him..."

"I know you do. I'm sorry too. I know you are under a lot of stress here at work."

"You wouldn't believe it." I rubbed my neck. My eyes turned back to her and I smirked, "I like your outfit."

"Really? I wore it for you."

"You did?" I chuckled. "Why?"

She shrugged and stood out of her chair. "I wanted to make things better for you. I figured, I could help ease some of that stress..." she hiked up her dress revealing that she didn't have any panties on and I bit my lip.

"Hannah..."

She didn't stop, and she leaned forward to kiss my neck. Her hand slid down my button down shirt, to my slacks. She unbuckled my belt and slipped her hand into my pants, slowly jerking me off.

"Hannah, we shouldn't..."

"It feels like you want this. You're hard."

"I do want this, but not here."

"You have an office. The door is closed. The blinds are closed. No one will know what we are doing. I can be quiet."

She kneeled in front of me and shimmied my pants around my ankles. She took my by the mouth and I gasped.

"Hannah...wait..." I groaned, feeling her tongue wrap around my length.

"What?" She innocently asked looking up at me.

"We can't do this..."

"It's okay, baby. It's just a quickie."

"Hannah, stop. There's people in here."

"So?"

"Hannah!" I pushed her away, and her eyes opened wide staring at me. She let out a frustrated sigh.

"Seriously, what is wrong with you?"

" I'm sorry, I really want to fuck you. Trust me. I'm so fucking hard for you right now, but I can't right now. I'm sorry."

Hannah shook her head. "What happened to us?" she chuckled and stood up. Placing her palm on her forehead she growled. "Damn…what happened to us?" She repeated. "You know there used to be a time when you would've had your way with me. You would've, slammed me against the table and fucked me until I was dripping with your cum, but now, what? What's our relationship now? A quick fuck every Friday or something? This isn't the man I fell in love with . You're not Deshawn. You're someone else. "

She lowered her skirt and adjusted her top. Taking another breath she glared at me. "I'm starting to learn there's a reason why your relationships always fizzled out. There's no commitment. You don't care."

"Hannah I do care…"

She shook her head and walked away.

"Hannah, wait! I do care. I DO CARE!" I yelled, but she didn't turn back.

She held her head up and stomped out of my office. Once she was gone, I growled and slammed the door shut.

"Son of a bitch!" I cried. I shoved the papers off my desk and fell to the floor.

I didn't care who heard me. I didn't give a fuck anymore. What was the point of living if she wasn't in my life. My world felt like it was a bit darker. The air seemed like it was harder to breath. My head was spinning and I was crashing but there was no where to land.

All I wanted to do was cry, but I couldn't. Nothing was coming out. Why couldn't I cry?

I sat on the floor holding my knees when there was a knock at me door.

"Not now..." I snapped.

"Deshawn it's, Tony, you got a moment?"

"Yeah, some in..."

Tony opened the door and his eyes opened wide, staring at the papers on the floor and then he saw me sitting.

"Everything, okay?"

"Yeah, I'm sure the whole office heard us."

"Yeah. Just about..." he chuckled. "How bout you get off the floor and talk to me."

I sighed and stood up, my pants were still unzipped and were opened.

Tony chuckled looking at my clothes, and pointed to my pants, "you might want to zip up son. You're showing everything."

"Shit..." I muttered, tucking my shirt in and zipping up my slacks. "Thanks."

"No, problem. So why did that fine ass Hannah come walking into your office looking the way that she did?"

"What you think?" I asked.

He chuckled. "Ah, looking to come by and pop that office cherry. I still remember the day Vicki popped mine. She still likes to come by every now and again and play secretary. How was it?"

"We didn't do anything."

"You didn't do anything!" He scoffed. "With her fine ass looking like that, you didn't do nothing?"

"Nah, I told her I wanted too, but I was too busy."

"Busy with what?"

"Work. Nick is driving me insane with these projects."

"Listen, take it from a old timer like me. If your woman wants to have sex. You drop everything and you have sex with her. Nothing trumps sex. Trust me. Women like Hannah and like my Vicki are a dime a dozen. Those woman get men like us with high sex drives. There's a reason why a lot of your relationships don't work out because the women you're with can't match your pace. You're a sports car and they're a mini van. Hannah, however, is a sports car, too and she can go the distance with you, if you give her a chance. This work will be here tomorrow..."

"But..."

Tony held up his hand and shook his head. "Don't worry about Nick. I'll speak with him. If he's still busting your balls, you'd come work in my division. You need a work life balance. The prick has to understand that. Work is temporary, but Hannah's love for you isn't. Don't waste it. Whatever the problem, fix it and fix it fast."

I smirked and nodded. "Thanks for the talk, Tony. I gotta go."

"Where are you going? It's not even five yet?"

"I'm going to go get my girl. The work can wait."

He chuckled. "Good, talk. Good talk. I'll catch you later?"

"Yeah, definitely..." I smiled, running out the door.

Chapter 22

I drove as fast as I could back to the townhouse. When I arrived, I ran inside, shouting, "Hannah!"

I found her sitting on the couch, she was crying, wiping her eyes with a tissue.

"What are you doing home so early?" She sobbed. Her eyes were red and puffy as she looked into mine.

I sat on the couch next to her and held her hand. "I came home early to say that I'm sorry. I'm sorry I put the work first. I'm sorry I made you feel this way. I've spoken to to Tony and he's going to talk to my boss about lightening the load. I should be more available now. I'm so sorry..."

I hugged her and rubbed her back.

"That's good..." she sniffed. She sighed and wiped her eyes.

"Hannah...what's wrong? I thought you'd be happy about this?"

She got up and walked into the bathroom before returning back to me with something in her hands.

"These last few days, I've felt off. I've been nauseous and moody, and at first I thought it was because we were fighting, but..." she revealed the pregnancy test to me and gave me a small smile.

"It's actually because I'm pregnant."

My jaw dropped, staring back at her.

She chuckled. "All this time I've been careful. I've always told you to wear a condom, and as soon as I let my guard down, I get knocked up within a couple of months. Fuck...Deshawn. I know we have our problems right now, and having a baby ain't what we need right now. I don't know what you want to do with this baby but..."

I slid off the sofa and got on one knee.

"Deshawn, what are you doing?" She asked.

I pulled out the ring in my back pocket and she gasped.

"Deshawn....what are you doing?" She repeated breathless.

"I'm marrying you. If you'll allow me. I want to be with you Hannah. I had a long talk with Tony and he made me realize that there are more things in life important that work. You say that this relationship will fizzle out. I disagree. I won't let it fizzle out. I won't let you go. You'd have to kill me to get rid of me. I'm not going anywhere. This ring..." looked down at the gold banded diamond.

"Is not only a symbol of my love for you, but also a commitment from me. This ring I promise I will not abandon you. Yes, we may have our fights here and there, but I will always come back to you. I will always love you. No matter what life throws at us. I will be there. I will be there for you. Work, Thomas, this baby, it doesn't matter. I will be there. I fucking love you Hannah. I love you with all my heart. I love you so much it fucking hurts. Will you marry me?"

Hannah doesn't say a thing as she looked at me and then towards the ring.

"Hannah, I..."

Before I could say another word she jumped on top of me, pushing me on the ground. She straddled my waist, and rubbed my cock making me hard.

I didn't know what her answer was, but I knew I wanted her. I wanted all of her.

As we kissed, we shed our clothes, becoming naked and she sat on my hard dick, riding me like she's always done before. I laid on the ground watching as the goddess took me.

"Does this mean, yes?" I groaned feeling her magical wetness around me.

"What do you think..." she smirked, leaning down to kiss me once more.

Just like the first time we had sex, she had me in her web. She was mine, and I didn't want to leave her. That online hookup was just supposed to be a one time thing. It wasn't supposed to lead to this. It wasn't supposed to lead to me having a wife, an adopted son, or daughter, but it did.

My life turned upside down since that night and I never regretted since. Hannah was my wife. She was mine. She was all fucking mine.

Don't miss out!

Visit the website below and you can sign up to receive emails whenever Hunter Briggs publishes a new book. There's no charge and no obligation.

https://books2read.com/r/B-A-SGQJB-PHGID

Connecting independent readers to independent writers.

Also by Hunter Briggs

An Erotic Interracial Romance
Taken by a Black Man: The Asian BBW
My Filipino Wife

Standalone
I Think My Neighbor is a Hooker
The African Samurai's Consort
Online Hookup: A Curvy WWBM Spicy Romance

About the Author

Hunter Briggs is an interracial romance erotica author. He loves writing out of the box stories, that at are different from the rest. If you like reading about tall, dark and handsome alphas and beautiful, thick thighed women, then Hunter Briggs is the author for you. If he's not writing hot, burn a hole in your panties erotica, Hunter Briggs is lazily watching TV because he has no other cool hobbies like other authors. Hunter Briggs is a loving husband and father and while he owns no dogs, he has always wished for a furry friend. He enjoys anything that can raise his blood pressure including, spicy buffalo wings, onion rings and ice-cold beer.

Follow me on Twitter: @Briggs_Romance

Milton Keynes UK
Ingram Content Group UK Ltd.
UKHW011814120624
444110UK00001B/52